The Beauty of Magic

The Beauty of Magic

Rachel Ann Michael Harris

The Beauty of Magic

To all women,
remember that beauty is more than skin deep.

Proverbs 31:30

Chapter 1

GREEN LIGHTNING FLASHED, crawling across the floor and up the walls until it danced upon the ceiling. King Alric convulsed before collapsing dead at Queen Maj's feet. With a wide grin, she leaned her head back, hands held out, lightning bursting from her fingertips as she cackled.

Svana swung away from the doorway as a bolt shot through it into the corridor she stood in. Breaths coming in gasps, she pressed her back against the stone wall as she blinked.

Father. She just killed Father.

Across the door from her, Bjorn flattened himself against the wall as well, his face a mirror of her shock, his eyes wide and mouth hanging open.

That woman couldn't get away with this. As Svana reached into her boot for a knife, Bjorn jumped from his place and grabbed her wrist. Svana twisted her arm, but he wouldn't let go.

"No." His eyes were wide as he gripped her wrist. With the lightning still blazing, he didn't even try to keep his voice down as he pulled her away. "You are the only thing standing between her and the crown. You have to run. Now."

Svana glanced back to the door.

"She'll be here any second. You can't fight her magic."

Hesitating, Svana nodded. Bjorn grasped her hand and dragged her down the hall, away from the still cackling queen.

They raced around corners and down the empty corridors, the servants tending to matters elsewhere or preparing the evening meal. As they ran, she thought of the green lightning. *How long had Maj been able to use magic? Why would she kill Father?*

They charged down another corridor toward a side door. While Bjorn stopped and peeked outside, Svana glanced over her shoulder, considering going back. The green lightning sparked in her mind's eye. Bjorn was right. She couldn't just fight Maj. How would she stop someone with magic anyways?

Pushing the wooden door open, Bjorn and Svana ran through the stable yard and into the barn.

Their horses were still saddled from their afternoon ride. Svana leapt into Tindra's saddle as Bjorn grabbed her bow and arrows and gave them to her before jumping onto his own horse. Svana strapped the quiver to her back but kept the bow in her hand. They raced the horses out of the stable, their hooves pounding the ground, drumming like thunder through the yard toward the gate.

"Stop them!" Maj's voice rang out across the yard.

Svana lay against Tindra's neck as they charged out the gate.

"NO!" echoed from Castle Alwilda's yard in a high-pitched screech as green light tinted the sky above.

Galloping, they charged through the village toward the woods. As they broke through the first stand of trees, Svana slowed down.

"Don't stop," Bjorn said. "They could be following us."

A sound, like whispering voices, chattered and grated through the air. Behind them, a plume of green smoke with flashing light wove down the path they'd ridden, the chattering growing louder.

Svana choked on the air as she gripped her reins.

"Run," said Bjorn. "RUN!"

They turned their horses deeper into the woods and fled. Over the years, they'd spent more time in the forest and its secret paths like an unmarked labyrinth than they had in the castle grounds. Svana tugged her horse's reins, making sharp turns around trees in hopes of eluding the cloud. They ducked under low branches before jumping over a fallen log. After Tindra landed, Svana glanced back. The cloud continued to follow, leaving a wispy trail. Nothing seemed to hinder it.

Lying against her horse's neck, Svana felt the slick foam on Tindra's neck. Her own hands were sweating and slipping on the reins. If they kept going like this, Tindra would either slow or injure a leg. Then they would be caught. Svana looked back again and saw the green smoke on their tails. But it wasn't coming after her.

Bjorn turned to her, seeing it too. He flicked his reins several times but it didn't matter. The smoke was right behind him.

"No matter what happens," he said, "keep going! Keep—"

Bjorn cringed as the green smoke settled around his head. He grimaced and clenched his jaw as it absorbed into him. Then he relaxed. Slowly, his head turned toward her. But his eyes…it was like something was clouding them. Taking his bow, he reached for an arrow, nocked it, and aimed in her direction.

Svana dodged to the right, swerving around a tree and away from Bjorn. The arrow flew behind her. Veering around trees, Svana avoided the next five arrows as they flew above her head or skimmed behind her.

Then one grazed Tindra's breast.

Tossing her head back, Tindra whinnied and stumbled sideways. Svana gripped the saddle horn to keep her seat as the horse thrashed. In moments, she settled from Svana's clucks and soothing strokes.

Bjorn shot past and Svana took the opportunity to duck to the left and around some pines. When she glanced back, he'd wheeled around and was pursuing them while nocking another arrow.

As he drew the arrow back, he rode up beside her, within arm's reach. His bow shook from the jostling ride and the strain of holding the string too long. Before he could release, Svana grasped her bow and swung the end, smacking him in the face as they passed. He crumpled and his shot went off into the woods as his horse slowed.

Why'd he waited to shoot till we were so close?

Svana glanced back as Bjorn turned his horse around, galloping in her direction until they were parallel. Reaching into his boot, he pulled a knife.

Svana put an arrow to her bow. Lifting it, she aimed toward Bjorn. Tindra's stride made it difficult to stay steady as she swayed with her gait. When she looked at Bjorn, she saw no recognition in his eyes. He didn't even seem human.

Pulling the bowstring past her cheek, Svana took a deep breath and released.

The arrow sank into a tree inches from Bjorn's horse's chest. The horse whinnied and reared, thrashing its hooves, throwing Bjorn to the ground.

As Svana took the reins again, she closed her eyes, shutting them tight and biting her lip. Then she turned back.

Bjorn got up, moving one arm or leg at a time. When he finally stood again, he watched her race away, making no effort to pursue. Turning her attention to the forest ahead, Svana flew around trees and shrubs as loose strands of her gold hair stung her eyes. A lump rose in her throat and tears wetted her face. Gasping, she clutched the reins and laid her head on Tindra's neck as they raced away from her home and closest friend.

Hours of traversing woods, gullies, and ditches later, Svana and Tindra trudged through the tree line to the edge of a cliff. Svana sat slumped in the saddle and Tindra had a lather like sea foam on her neck and back. With the back of her hand, Svana swept away wisps of her sweat-soaked hair then dismounted. Inching toward the precipice, she looked down.

It was a sheer drop with only a couple of branches reaching through cracks in the cliff's face. A river ran below like a pure, blue ribbon that was dropped on the floor. It must have been the Jeneve River, flowing from the northern mountains to Loch Linux two-to-three days' journey away. Across the river, pines and brown rocks dotted the forest with no end in sight. The sun was setting, casting the forest into pockets of black and orange-red. She had to find a place to hide and continue in the morning.

But where am I even supposed to go?

Growling, Svana kicked the dirt. The gravelly cloud settled around her horse's hooves. Small sparks like embers blinked as dust settled around one of Tindra's back legs. Svana gently kicked a bit of dirt toward it. The air around the ankle sparked again. Running a hand along Tindra's side, Svana knelt and blew toward the hoof. Green flecks caught the light surrounding the horse's fetlock.

Scrambling back, Svana spun around, glancing at every tree and shadow. Could Maj track her through magic? She had no idea.

What now? Svana scanned the cliff then the forest.

Tossing the reins over the Tindra's head, Svana pointed the horse back into the trees and rubbed her nose, feeling her heavy breaths. "Sorry, girl. I need you to go a little longer."

She slapped the horse's hindquarters, chasing her into a gallop. "Yah!"

Tindra tossed her head and bolted into the forest.

As she disappeared, Svana grimaced, watching the last of her allies vanish. *What will Maj do when she finds her?* Taking a deep breath, she turned away and focused on the problem at hand.

She returned to the cliff, kneeling down to examine the face closer. Among the cracks and crags, she noticed a rough, narrow path leading to the river below. Wide enough to descend, narrow enough to fall with one wrong step. Swinging her legs over the edge, she leaned her back against the cliff and descended sideways. As she inched her way down, rocks and dirt knocked loose from her feet and hands, skittering below.

"Brilliant idea, Svana." She clenched her jaw with each step but kept going. When she reached the bottom, she bolted away from the cliff. Taking one more look at it, she was glad to leave it behind.

The bank was made of stones and boulders up to the river that flowed past with gentle gurgles. Svana stumbled toward it and knelt, cupping water into her dirt-covered hands, and drank. After tossing some water on the back of her neck, she glanced around. The stream was wide and swift but shallow, full of trout who were leaping upstream around boulders that dotted the surface. If she wanted to cross, she could either wade through or hop boulder-to-boulder. She sighed and rubbed her face, too tired to try either now. The sun sank lower, turning everything a shade of black.

Reluctantly turning back to the cliff, Svana saw a black hole in its side. Wondering if it was a trick of the light, she scrambled over the rocky terrain and found a cave entrance. She staggered inside, the last of the fading light outside enough to see piles of leaves down its length and—neatly laid out on stones as if drying—fish which still had scales and large eyes that seemed to follow her as she walked past.

Well, whoever lives here, I hope they won't mind a guest.

The leaf piles were mixed with dirt and formed into circles. Svana guessed they were beds. *Who sleeps on leaves? Or lives in a cave for that matter.* Too tired to think it through, she wandered inside and started examining the beds.

Sitting in the first one, she was poked in the back by stems and twigs. Someone either had been very lazy building this or didn't mind getting scratched. She quickly scrambled out and brushed off leaves that stuck to her green hunting dress.

In the next one, she sank several inches and threw up her hands in surprise. They had built up their pile of leaves so thick that she was half buried. It took a minute to stand back up which scattered the leaves all over the ground.

The next several weren't much better. Too flat. Too tall. Branches lined up in little lines resembling a raft. One was just a circle of rocks with the hard, stone floor in the center. She shook her head as she passed it.

When she made it to the seventh pile, she was ready to pass out and didn't take time to test it. She unstrung her bow out of habit then collapsed on the bed. It was perfect.

The leaves were nicely laid out to create a down-feather-like feel and yet was cushier than the others. Her hand felt cool, rich soil and she realized the extra comfort was churned dirt mixed in with leaves. Curling in deeper, Svana closed her eyes.

The cave grew dark as the sun set. It reminded her of when she was little and of her father's seven lords. Lord Olin reading to her at bedtime. Or Lord Dahl sneaking her an extra biscuit at dinner, much to his own sadness. He loved biscuits too. Or Lord Magnar. He'd been a father to her when her own hadn't. Images of green lightning and her father collapsing flashed through her mind. She closed her eyes and rolled over but the sight of Bjorn's glassy eyes and fierce face when that smoke consumed him was all she could see.

Father was dead. Bjorn under an enchantment. And the lords gone, disappearing one-by-one over the last few years.

As exhaustion began to win over the haunting events of the afternoon, her mind drifted back to her childhood and when her world started to crumble because of the only mother she had ever known.

Svana ran down the corridor, giggling, her golden hair a braided circlet with ribbons and flowers woven throughout with loose strands cascading behind her. Turning the corner, she skidded to a stop before her mother's chamber door and straightened her tartan dress before entering. Sitting before a table with a mirror hanging over it, Queen

Maj brushed her silky black hair, letting it drape down her back. Svana walked up and leaned against her lap.

"You are beautiful, Mother," Svana said.

Her mother looked down and removed Svana's small hands from the skirt of her emerald-green dress. "Now, what have I told you? You'll wrinkle it." She returned her attention to the mirror.

"Sorry, Mother." Svana took a step back. "I hope I'm just as beautiful as you someday."

Her mother continued to brush her hair. "Thank you, dear," she said then stood. "Come. We must go." Folding her hands in front of her, the queen led Svana out of the room.

Svana tried to copy her but couldn't keep her hands still and walked more with a stomp instead of graceful glides.

After traversing several corridors and descending a flight of stairs, they reached Castle Alwilda's large, wooden doors. King Alric and Lord Magnar, her father's closest friend and advisor, talked as they waited to process out to watch the games. Six other lords waited behind them in a rough line. Lord Axel leaned against a wall, stifling a yawn as Lord Dane animatedly described one of his grand adventures to Lord Henrik. Henrik didn't seem very impressed with the tale but young Vidar, lord-to-be, hung on every word with wide eyes. Lord Olin was shaking his head at Lord Henrik's spectacle while Lord Dahl tried sneaking one more treat before the festivities began. They were a grand sight in their livery. Svana ran ahead, smiling at her father.

"Papa." Svana jumped into his arms.

King Alric caught and lifted her above his head as she giggled. "Oh, there is my little swan."

"Now, my husband. You'll spoil her." The queen took Svana from him and set her on the ground behind her.

"Of course, my queen," he said, smiling as he leaned down to kiss her mother.

Svana waited, bouncing on her toes, for him to look at her again, but the king kept his eyes on the queen's, holding her hands, and leaned his head against hers.

Lord Magnar knelt down before Svana. "Ready to see your people, little one?"

Svana shook her hair from her face. "I'm not little anymore. I'm eight now."

Lord Magnar held up his hands and gave an exaggerated bow. "Oh, forgive me, Your Highness."

She gave a little curtsy. "You're forgiven, my lord." Spinning around, she let her skirt flare around her. "Aren't I beautiful? Like magic!"

Magnar frowned and held up his finger. "No, dear, not like magic. That is not something to joke about or play with."

"Is it bad?"

With a sideways glance, Mother watched the discussion between them but didn't interject.

Pursing his lips, Magnar glanced to one of the other lords.

Quickly clearing his throat, Lord Olin shifted under Magnar's stare then knelt down. His face was somber as he said, "I've seen magic before. It…" At a loss for words, he glanced at his fellow lords. "It is not something to play with. It can be…misused."

Svana scrunched her nose. "How?"

Lord Olin opened his mouth, gestured with his hand, but didn't say anything.

To save him, Vidar leaned toward her, twisting his face in a funny, grotesque position and said, "Because it belongs to old, sour hags who will muddle your mind and eat you."

The queen rolled her eyes and shook her head.

But Svana giggled and pushed him away before jumping on Lord Magnar's back.

"Svana!" Her mother glared at her. Behind Mother, her father also frowned. The corridor was silent.

Svana crawled down. "Sorry, Mama."

Her mother spun toward the doors, wrapping her arm around the king's. He patted the queen's hand and faced the doors with her. The herald outside began their introductions.

Svana sniffed and wiped her nose on her sleeve.

Lord Magnar lowered his hand to her. "May I escort you out, Princess Svana?"

Curtsying, she smiled. "I would be pleased, Lord Magnar."

The herald announced, "King Alric, with his wife, Queen Maj, and daughter, Princess Svana, of Tyra," loudly for all to hear as the doors opened, letting the sun blaze upon them as they stepped out and bagpipes blared.

The large, grassy field was filled with people in their finest clothes as colorful flags and booths dotted the landscape. But it was the games prepared across the lawn, challenging participants' might and finesse, that Svana couldn't wait to watch. Stones as big as a man's head to be tossed, logs three times their height to be thrown, and tug-of-war to prove a group's strength.

A pavilion with two large chairs and one small one stood on the far side of the field, allowing the royal family to sit and watch the festivities in comfort. Magnar walked up the steps of the pavilion and held Svana's hand as she took her seat before bowing and taking his position to the side.

Archers prepared their bows and tested their strings for the first competition. Right in front of the pavilion was the village hunter and his son who was about a year or so older than Svana. She knew him from when he sold his game at the castle. The hunter never seemed to notice her but his son would glance her way and wave on occasion. She always smiled and waved back. What was his name? She waited to catch his eye now but he never looked away from helping his father. As she watched, the boy strung the bow and handed it to his father. Her eyes widened at his strength and she thought perhaps he should compete in some of the events.

People gathered to watch. In front of the pavilion, a couple of women glanced up at the royal family.

One of them whispered to the other, "Look at Princess Svana. With all that golden hair and bright eyes."

"Beautiful," said the other.

The first one leaned close to her companion. "As beautiful as her mother, our queen."

The second smiled and nodded.

Svana squirmed and grinned. *As beautiful as her mother.* She turned to the queen to tell her, but leaned back when she saw her mother's face, her smile fading.

Why did Mother look so angry?

Chapter 2

BJORN RODE INTO the stable yard as the sun disappeared behind Castle Alwilda. Dismounting, he dropped the reins in a servant's hand without giving them a glance, marched toward the large, double doors leading into the great hall, and pushed them open.

Inside, Queen Maj stood upon a raised dais, stroking the curved edge of a standing oval mirror. She gazed at herself, examining her face framed by loose, black hair, and straightening her green-and-black gown in the reflection. When Bjorn was halfway to the dais, she looked at the edge of the mirror. Halting, he knelt before her.

"Well, I had hoped you would have brought Svana back with you." Tossing the train of her skirts behind her, Maj sauntered toward him. "I thought your hunting skills were better." She circled him. As she came to face him again, she took his chin in her hand and raised his chin. "Shame."

She slapped him.

Bjorn didn't blink.

Pursing her lips, Maj returned to her mirror and stroked it. "Mirror, mirror, heed unto me, show me Svana's steed."

Green smoke circled within the glass. The queen's reflection was replaced with blurred tan-and-green images. With a huff, Queen Maj waved her hand at the mirror. The colors slowed and smoothed into shapes of distant mountains and scraggly trees. Grass obscured the view but the legs of Svana's horse were clear.

"She's in the Dyre Fields by the Eiwyn Mountains." Another wave and the mirror returned to normal. "Come, let us retrieve the princess." The queen strode past Bjorn toward the hall doors as a green flame flared around her hand like a torch.

Bjorn rose. He stood for a moment, staring at the mirror across the room before following, his body moving of its own accord. A tear rolled down his cheek.

Dry leaves scratched Svana's face. They crinkled and shredded beneath her as she shifted, still half asleep but her mind returning to the real world. Above, a puff of hot air tossed loose strands of her hair.

Someone's home. Slowly, she opened her eyes, her vision filled with the large nose of an even larger brown bear.

It tilted its head to the side.

"Rawr." Its maw opened wide, displaying dagger-sharp white teeth.

Svana gasped. She rolled and scrambled for her bow. The bear stumbled backward in surprise as it let out a louder *rawr.*

Springing to her knees and with no time to string it, Svana lifted her bow like a staff and swung it down squarely between its eyes.

The beast shook its head and gruffed. Plopping on its tail, it rubbed the spot between its ears.

Svana brought the bow back to swing again but hesitated. *Bears don't sit back and rub their heads in pain.*

Lifting his head, the bear scrunching its brow and tipped its head to the side. Svana copied him.

Behind it, six more bears of various shapes and sizes filled the cave. They were looking at her with lopsided heads and dropped jaws or each turning to one of its neighbors with wide eyes. These bears were acting too… human.

Shaking his head, the one Svana hit dropped to his front paws and took a step toward her. She lifted the bow slightly and gritted her teeth, ready to strike again.

He lifted a paw as if gesturing to wait.

She nearly dropped her bow. *What's going on?*

With a sweep of his paw, he brought it to his chest and bowed, which the other bears copied.

"All right?" Svana lowered the bow a bit more.

The bear turned and grunted to the others who returned to their previous tasks. As they moved about the cave, they kept glancing at her. The one before her jerked his head toward the cave mouth and walked toward it. Biting her cheek, she hesitated then grabbed her quiver and followed.

As she walked past, she watched the bears as they settled about the cave. Several went to their beds and lay down. One bear went to the bed that had nearly swallowed her and dropped his jaw. The lose skin of his jowls swung back and forth as he swung his head, examining the leaves in disarray, before wailing in dismay. Unable to drown out the noise, several of the others roared back at him and covered their ears. Hanging his head, he pawed the leaves back into their pile.

Grimacing, Svana watched the pitiful sight. Placing the bow on her back, she knelt down and scooped a large batch of leaves back into his pile.

"Sorry," she said.

The bear's sagging ears perked up a bit and he tossed the leaves back into their perfect circle with gusto. Once all the leaves were in place, the bear nodded before he ducked down and walked into the pile, disappearing within the mass. Soon, a couple of the leaves blew back and forth with the sound of snoring.

At the cave entrance sat a barrel of a bear, a pile of trout beside him and another squished between his paws. With slow and precise movements, he would take one from the pile and lay it down, fiddling with it until it was perfect. When the pile was depleted, he sat back and stared at them lying side by side. His shining eyes gazed at the rows. Slowly, his large tongue lolled out of his mouth, around a fish, and pulled it into his jaws.

Two others saw this and roared at him and tossed out their paws in frustration. Svana could almost hear the words. *What are you doing? Not again. You are supposed to be drying the fish, not eating them!*

The bear's ears drooped, and he lowered his head and spat out the bones.

Svana stepped over to him. Reaching out her hand, she slowly lowered it to his shoulder. He gazed at her with large, brown eyes. Still unsure, she stroked his fur.

He closed his eyes and the ends of his lips turned up as he sighed. The roly-poly bear nodded with a grunt before tossing his paws around her neck. As she fell, Svana's hand jerked to her knife, expecting his jaws to close around her face. Instead, his head butted into her neck like a nuzzle.

"Rawwwwr." The leader bear lumbered up behind them and batted at the larger one.

Letting go, the bulky bear walked around them, head low, before going into the cave.

The leader came over to her and nodded his head outside. The sun was breaking above the pines, casting a golden hue to the river. Svana settled on a rock and the bear sat down beside her.

She shook her head. "Who are you?"

The bear tipped his head, like he was considering her question. Holding up a paw, he ambled back into the cave. When he returned, he carried in his mouth a large swath of cloth, part of which dragged on the ground, and dropped it before her.

With her finger and thumb, Svana picked it up by the shoulders. It was a forest-green cloak with her father's crest. The garment of a lord.

"You ate them?!"

The bear jerked his head from side to side, almost twisting it around in a circle as he shook his head. Standing on his hind legs, the bear held up his head regally before giving a dramatic bow, almost toppling over as he lost his balance.

There was something about that overdramatic bow. She had seen it before. When she was a child…

"You…?" Svana looked down at the cloak again. In the cave were six bears and this one next to her. "Seven lords," she murmured. "Lord Magnar?"

The bear jerked his head up and down until his front paws lifted off the ground.

She tossed her arms around his neck and squeezed. His thick, rough fur engulfed her, warming her like a blanket before a fire.

"I thought you were lost." She burrowed her face into his neck, the weight of the last couple years with him gone lifting from her shoulders. "I thought you were killed by wolves or…" Svana was going to say bears but that didn't seem appropriate. Taking a step back, she examined his bulky frame.

Three years ago, Lord Magnar, and then each lord after him, had been sent on an emissary mission to a neighboring kingdom never to return.

"How…" Svana closed her eyes, not needing him to answer. "Maj. She did this, didn't she?"

Lord Magnar nodded again.

Maj. First, she discarded and cursed the king's lords, then she… Flashing green lightning and her father falling to the floor flared in Svana's mind. She gasped and clenched her eyes shut.

Magnar turned his head to the side and lowered his brows as he watched her.

How could she tell him? Magnar and her father had grown up together. Were like brothers. Magnar used to sit her on his knees and tell her stories of the adventures they had when they were young. Her favorite was when Magnar challenged her father to woo a cowherderess and her father stole his father's golden harp. He'd brought it down to the field and played it for her. Apparently, he played so badly she threw an egg at him before snatching the harp and playing it herself, catching the ear of a young man whom she would eventually marry. Magnar would roar every time he told that story.

This is going to break his heart. Holding his face between her hands, Svana looked into his big, brown eyes. "I have to tell you something." She stroked his fur then swallowed. "Father is dead. Killed by Maj."

Lord Magnar's mouth dropped and he stepped back. Grunting, he turned his head from side to side. Throwing it back, he roared until the forest and cliff rang with it, echoing back in a loop. Svana wrapped her arms around him. He dropped his head down her back, panting and whimpering as he trembled. His shaking rocked her to the core. His arm came around her shoulders as he huffed and whined.

As he cried, Svana squeezed her eyes shut as tears filled her eyes. Grasping his fur, she buried her head in his shoulder and mourned with Magnar.

Svana peeked into her mother's room. That fury during the games still haunted Svana. She didn't understand. Didn't Mother want Svana to be beautiful? Like her?

"You sent for me, Mother?" Svana said from the doorway.

The queen looked up from the papers on her desk and nodded. "Yes, child." Queen Maj picked up a basket on the floor beside her. "Would you do your mummy a favor and get some apples? Not the ones in the garden but the ones beside the river."

The river? In the forest? Alone?

"Will Lord Magnar go with me?" Svana asked, tangling and untangling her fingers together.

"Of course not. You're a big girl now. You can go yourself."

The thick trees towering over her filled Svana's mind. "But Papa said—"

"Are you going to disobey me?" The fire flickered in her eyes again.

Svana shook her head, her golden curls bouncing. "No." And took the basket.

"Good. Now run along." The queen waved her hand and turned back to her papers.

Svana hesitated, slowly walking away, glancing back every few steps, but the queen didn't look at her again.

What do I do? Father said never to go to the woods alone. But Mother asked for the apples by the river. Wringing her hands on the basket handle, Svana dragged her feet across the flagstones.

A boisterous laugh echoed down the corridor. She knew that voice. Svana smiled and ran around the corner.

Lord Dahl's plump stomach seemed to sway as he walked but it made him look more endearing than gluttonous. It also gave Svana a place to sit when he picked her up.

"Lord Dahl!" Svana skidded to a stop on the stones.

"Oh, my young lady." Lord Dahl swept his hand high above his head then low to the ground in an exaggerated bow. "How are you this fine morning?"

"Good, thank you." She curtsied.

"Where are you off to?"

"Mother asked me to fetch some apples from—"

"Oh, that's splendid!" Lord Dahl clapped his hands together. "Would you mind grabbing an extra one for me?"

"Um, of course. I was hoping you would come with—"

"Oh, I'm sorry, but I'm on a task for Lord Magnar. You know how he gets." With a pat on her head, he said, "Make sure mine is extra red," and continued down the corridor.

Should I ask again? Glancing back and forth, Svana considered going after Lord Dahl. But he was busy and didn't have time to help. And she might get in trouble for asking again or taking too long. After several deep breaths, she stopped by her room for her red cloak then walked down the corridor to the stairs that led to the large double doors.

As she reached the great hall, she wrapped the cloak around her shoulders and lifted the hood. With both hands, she grasped the large, metal ring and leaned back as she dragged open the door leading to the courtyard.

Two guards stood on either side of the entrance. They didn't look at her or ask any questions as she left but remained stiffly at their post. Like the statues of the old kings that circled the throne room. Then again, they might have been a little sick. Their faces had a strange, green tinge. Nodding her head in greeting, she walked past, not wanting to bother them.

A thick fog hovered above the ground, swirling in large poofs as she walked through. Svana started and looked to her right. Strange, it seemed like the fog had a green tinge, too. Wanting to be back inside but too scared of disappointing her mother, Svana snuck through a side gate, across a field, and hurried to the woods.

Chapter 3

TINDRA GRAZED IN an open field surrounded by snow-capped mountains in the far distance. Bjorn and Queen Maj dismounted at the edge of the woods leading into Dyre Fields. The long grass up to her knees, the queen strode into the field toward the horse. Bjorn followed behind, waiting for a command.

She grasped the reins and waved a hand at one of its hind legs where green mist dissipated. Tossing her head, Tindra stepped back, whites showing around her eyes. The queen tugged the horse's head down.

"Where is your precious girl?" she murmured. Queen Maj scanned the trees and grass like they would reveal their secrets to her. She spun back to the horse. "You'll have to tell me." Waving her hand between the horse's eyes, the queen pulled her hand back slowly. Mist floated from the horse's forehead to the queen. Tindra neighed, the sound more like a scream. The horse stomped in place, pulling back but unable to move.

The mist swirled into an oval disk between Tindra and the queen. Quick glimpses of images flowed into the oval, sharing everything the horse had seen. Svana had ridden hard and far, the forest flying by for miles. She made it to a gorge. After a moment, Svana skittered into sight, spooked by something. The horse turned and suddenly charged back the way they had come. The stream stopped and the horse dropped its head to the grass, panting hard.

Queen Maj gasped, her hand spasming. Shaking, she looked down and rubbed a spot on her wrist. One hand around the other, she looked about but the only ones present were Bjorn and two guards a short distance away. After a moment, the queen shook her head and raised her chin, showing no signs of distress.

"So, she discovered my little spell. I know that gorge." Queen Maj tossed the reins to Bjorn. "Take it with us." She marched back to her horse, gently rubbing the spot on her wrist with her thumb.

Bjorn took the reins and led Tindra toward their steeds. As they followed the queen, he lifted a trembling hand, placed it on Tindra's neck, and gave it a quick stroke before it fell back to his side.

Leaning against the cliff face, Svana watched the seven bears stand in the river, catching trout in their open maws one by one before tossing the fish to a companion on the shore who placed it in a nearby pile. It was still hard for her to believe that these brown bears were her father's lords. If it wasn't for their unusual behavior or how Dahl kept trying to snack on the fish that jumped into his mouth, she probably still wouldn't believe it.

Lord Magnar shook his head, his soaking brown fur scattering water and spraying a fellow lord, before wading to shore. He grunted to her as he lumbered out of the river. Svana picked her way over the rocks to the bank.

"Good fishing?" She grinned, one side of her mouth turning up.

Magnar grumbled deep in his throat.

Svana bit her lip, stifling a chuckle, as she sat on a rock. For a moment, it felt like her childhood again. The river gurgled as it flowed past and the trout leaped into the waiting mouths of the bears. She sighed as reality settled on her shoulders once more.

"I don't understand," Svana said. "She has everything. Why would she kill father? What could she gain from his death?" Shaking her head, she picked up a stone and picked at it. "Did you know she had magic?"

Magnar lifted a paw.

"Right." She scratched at a speck on the stone. "I didn't. But… looking back… I think I saw it. I just didn't know. Like that time with the apples. Remember that?"

He growled as his brow lowered and his lips pulled back, exposing his teeth.

Svana leaned back and pushed his snout. "Don't get mad with me." Turning the stone between her fingers, she thought of her stepmother, the green lightning flashing all around her. "That was also one of the last times he and I really talked. I mean…you know we talked, but not like fathers and daughters do. I haven't really spoken to him in…" Svana paused and counted her fingers. "Ten years? Has it really been that long?"

She looked Magnar in the eye but dropped her gaze immediately. "Is it…wrong I don't feel anything? I think I feel sad. Confused. Unsure what to do. But we've been so distant for so long, I don't know what to think about Father's death."

A low growl emitting from his throat, Magnar laid a paw on her shoulder and nudged her cheek with his snout. She smiled and wiped her eyes. "I guess what I miss most is missing all that time. And knowing we'll never have a chance now."

As a memory drifted into her mind, a smile grew on her lips. "We did actually spend some time talking. We were falconing and he turned to me and just started talking. I don't even remember what he said but it wasn't about the crown or the kingdom, it was just…him asking about me." She sniffed. "It was nice."

She clenched the stone in her fist. "First she took you, then she took father. And now she has Bjorn."

Tossing the stone into the river, she stood and began pacing. "I have to stop her. If she rules the kingdom with magic, what will happen to it? To the people who defy her? What will she make Bjorn do? But…I don't know how to compete with magic."

She stopped in front of Magnar. "Do you know anything?"

Magnar's face was scrunched in thought. He glanced back at the bears then at Svana before casting his head down. He knew something.

"What?"

A moment passed before he sighed and clambered to his feet. Making his way to the river's edge, he roared to the others. They stopped and turned to him. Lord Magnar spoke in short bursts of growls and grunts, like the regal lord giving his men orders. After a moment, he grunted with a nod and the lords nodded. Together, they waded farther into the river, headed for the opposite shore.

Magnar stepped alongside Svana and pointed to his back with his nose.

Svana paused than pointed at him. "Up?"

He nodded.

Grabbing a fistful of his matted fur, Svana climbed on. As she pulled on his hair, Magnar grunted.

"Sorry." Absentmindedly, she stroked his fur. "Where are we going?"

Chattering echoed from the cliff.

Svana froze then spun around.

Atop the plateau, Bjorn sat upon Tindra, a small jewelry box in his hand. Green smoke poured from it.

"Bjorn!"

The lords turned and roared, baring their teeth at him. Lord Dane ran toward the cliff, splashing through the water like he was on a quest to tear Bjorn apart.

"Lord Dane, no!" Svana reached out to stop him. "He's under an enchantment."

Magnar roared and jumped into the lord's path. Dane stopped, sliding on the wet stones of the riverbed. Growling and shifting back and forth, debating between dashing past Magnar or turning around, Dane gritted his teeth before shaking his head. He dove back into the river.

Springing forward, Magnar rushed into the river and began to swim to the far side. The water grew steadily deeper as they crossed. Midway, it reached Svana's shoulders and covered Magnar's body as he paddled furiously.

Svana glanced back. Bjorn hadn't moved but the green mist had flowed down the cliff face and was drifting toward the river.

Lumbering onto the far shore, Magnar sprinted into the trees with a rocking, leaping gait. Svana gripped fistfuls of his fur as she slid side-to-side on his slick hair.

Before they entered the tree line, Svana looked back once more but could no longer see Bjorn. The green mist weaved its way toward them.

"Magnar!"

He didn't look. Instead, he hunkered closer to the ground, taking longer, rocking strides.

The green mist descended on them, slithering along the dirt path as it flowed around their feet and rose up from the ground like the tide. Dane tossed his paws into the mist. It split around his paws and hovered around Svana. The green mist swirled, encircling her in giant puffs. For a moment, she couldn't see anything but green. Then she couldn't breathe.

The strings from her hood wrapped themselves around her throat, pulling tight. Gasping, she tried to pick them apart. They grew tighter. She smacked Magnar's shoulder.

Stop. Stop!

He ran faster.

Why wouldn't he stop? Her chest tightened until it felt like it couldn't expand and was squeezing her lungs.

Panic clouded her vision, obscuring anything more than a few inches from her face.

Hands flying between the strings and holding Magnar's fur, Svana couldn't loosen the threads and keep her seat at the same time. Her strength was failing. He jumped over a log. Svana caught a chunk of his brown fur, tumbling to the right, but held on.

Her hand hit something hard as she caught herself. *My knife.*

Grasping the handle, she pulled it from her belt and raised it to her throat. With tingling fingertips, Svana tried to get the blade under but between Magnar's lumbering run and the string cutting into her skin, she couldn't get it close without stabbing herself.

The world was growing black and fuzzy around the edges of her vision. She gagged and hacked. Clawing at the strings, she picked at them in desperation with her fingernails. They grew tighter.

Magnar roared and leaped. And the strings loosened a finger's width. Svana slipped the knife beneath, the metal cold on her throat, and sliced the threads.

She choked as she heaved in air. Lying against Magnar, she brushed his coat as his pace slowed. He glanced back at her, his large brown eyes glistening with concern. Nodding, she wrapped her fingers in his fur again as he continued down the tree-lined path.

This is the third time I almost died in the woods. The world spinning and her throat burning where the strings had cinched around it, her mind drifted back to the first time.

It was a long trek across the golden wheat fields, the stalks taller than she was. When Svana reached the edge of the forest, she looked up. The trees towered above, reaching steadfast and straight into the sky. Deep inside, the green boughs loomed overhead, blocking out the sun and casting the woods in shadow. Gripping her basket, she walked in.

After several paces, she was consumed by the trees' shadow. It was dim but not totally black as she'd thought. More like the dim of a rising storm. Still, it felt strange. And quiet.

A branch broke. Svana gasped and whipped around as a deer leapt away across the forest floor. Hugging the basket to herself, she hurried on. The faster she got the apples, the faster she could go home.

"Ooh, ooh!"

"Ah!" Svana whipped around as a great, grey owl spread its wings and flew over her. Like she was being hunted. It glided up into the branches and disappeared. After a few moments, she continued on with cautious steps.

The path rose slightly as it led to a tree with a root sticking up out of the ground. As she stepped over it, a raven shot up and past her face.

"Caw!" it screamed.

Svana tripped backward and landed on her back. She scanned the trees but the raven had flown off.

With shaking hands, she grabbed her basket once again. It wasn't far to the river. Just one apple—two so

Lord Dahl could have one—and then she could go home. She had forgotten how long a trek it was.

Edging up to the tree again, she glanced around before darting to the next. The wind blew gently, scattering and rustling the dead leaves. She caught her breath and dug her fingers into the bark.

"Coo," trilled a dove perched on a branch above.

While Svana loved doves, she screamed before stopping to see what made the sound and ran headlong into the woods.

Her breaths came in panicked pants. She jumped over a fallen branch and glanced back. Then to the right. Back to front.

"Arroo!"

What was that? Her foot caught on a root and she tumbled to the ground, her hands digging into the dirt and sticks.

Svana crawled over to a tree and leaned against its trunk, hugging her knees to her chin. Gasping for breath, she watching the shifting shadows, listened to the sporadic crack of sticks or chitter of squirrels, waiting for the next attack. A whimper burst from her lips as tears ran down her face in a flood.

Her hands stung and the forest laughed at her as the trees' leaves rustled. Nothing was there and she was jumping at shadows. Lifting her head, she looked at her hands and her muddied dress. Mother would be angry.

She had trusted Svana to just fetch some apples, but she was scared of the breeze. It was a simple task. She could do it.

Wiping her eyes, Svana stood and dusted off her skirt. Her basket lay a few feet away, slightly crushed from where she'd fallen on it. *Mother will be angry about that, too.* Picking it up, she hugged it to herself and turned around.

"Rrrrrr." A wolf rounded the trunk of the tree she had sat under, baring its teeth as its eyes glowed an unnatural green.

"Ahhh!" Svana screamed.

The wolf snapped its jaws and lunged toward her.

She swung the basket and hit him on the snout.

Whimpering, the wolf stumbled to the side in shock.

Svana ran. Around trunks and under branches, moving her arms and legs as fast as she could as growls rumbled behind her.

Which way is home? Which way is home? The trees all looked the same.

"Arf! Arf!" the wolf barked. She could almost feel his breath.

The ground fell away under her and Svana fell into a gully.

The wolf braced his legs as he stopped at her feet. Growling, he lifted his head back as he opened his jaws.

"Aaaaaaahhhhhhh!"

An arrow pierced the wolf's throat. Its head jerked back then it fell over.

A hand grasped Svana's arm and pulled her away. It was a boy. The boy from the archery contest. He held a knife in one hand as he dragged her back with the other.

The boy's father ran past them to the wolf. "Dead," he said. He turned to Svana and walked over to her. "Are you all right, dear?"

She whimpered. Her arms wouldn't stop shaking.

"Are you hurt?" he asked.

She shook her head.

He glanced around them. "Where are your parents?"

She scrunched her eyes closed and cried.

"It's all right, dear." The hunter picked her up and rubbed her back. "Let's get you out of these woods."

Sobbing, Svana laid her head on his shoulder and hugged his neck. "Apples."

He stopped. "What?"

"I have to get apples for Mother. She'll be mad if I don't."

"It's all right," he said as he patted her shoulder. "We'll buy some in the village."

"No." Svana shook her head, her face soaked from tears. "She wanted them from the river."

"What parent sends a child into the woods for apples?" he muttered.

"Here." The boy reached into his pack and removed three apples. "I picked them this morning."

Svana glanced at her empty arms and began crying again. "I lost my basket."

The hunter patted her back and turned to the boy. "You carry them." But he took one and held it out to her. "Here, have one. It'll make you feel better."

Svana took it but didn't eat it. She gazed at the red apple and turned it around in her hands as the hunter and boy walked. When they stepped out of the woods, the sun warmed her face. She sniffed and lifted her head from his shoulder. "I think Lord Dahl will like this one."

"Lord Dahl?" The hunter hesitated. "You live in Castle Alwilda?"

Svana nodded.

"That makes things much easier," he said.

As they strode through the streets, Svana noticed how clear things seemed to be. The strange fog from when she departed seemed to have lifted, leaving a bright, sunny day.

As they approached the castle gates, there was a slight stir before a man in bright livery burst through the gate and drew his sword.

"Put her down or I'll chop you to pieces and feed you to the dogs!"

She knew that fiery temper that made squires and nobles quake. "Lord Dane!" Svana wiggled down and ran to the lord, wrapping her arms around his legs.

"Please." The hunter lowered himself to his knees, pulling the boy down with him. "We found her wandering in the woods and wanted to bring her home."

"They saved me from the big, scary dog," Svana said.

"Where have you been, dear girl? We have been tearing the castle apart for you."

"She was in the woods, my lord," the hunter said.

Lord Dane lifted his sword. "Hold your tongue or I'll cut it off."

"I was in the woods." Svana tugged on Dane's arm.

He looked from her to the hunter. "Who are you?"

"A simple hunter, my lord. I am called Arvid, and this is my son, Bjorn."

Dane squinted at them, a gaze that seemed to see through the skin to the very heart and soul. Replacing his sword, he jerked his chin to the soldiers behind him.

Soldiers along the battlements armed with bows lowered their weapons.

Dane nodded his head inside. "Come with me." He picked up Svana. "We need to discuss this further."

"But she did. She sent me to the woods to get apples," Svana insisted to her father.

He rubbed his eyes and sighed. "Why would Maj do that when we have perfectly good apples in the garden?"

"Because she liked the ones in the woods better."

King Alric leaned down to her. "Dear, you were mistaken."

"No." Svana had told her father the story so why didn't he believe her? "Please, Papa."

All seven lords were spread around the room. The hunter and his son stood in the back corner out of the way. They looked one to the other, shrugging and shaking their heads.

Don't any of them believe me?

The door opened and Maj walked in.

"Child, what happened to you?" She ran across the room and took Svana's hand.

Svana grasped her hands. "Tell Papa. Tell him you sent me to the woods to get apples."

Dropping Svana's hand, Maj placed hers over her heart. "Whatever would I do that for? I asked you to fetch me an apple but not from the woods."

"But…" Svana looked to her father and the lords. "But you said they were your favorite. You said you wanted those."

"I said nothing of the sort." Maj turned to King Alric. "I explicitly told her not to go into the woods."

What? "You did not!" Svana screamed and stomped her foot.

"Svana! Do not speak to your mother that way," the king scolded.

"Child, do not lie just because you were confused and made a mistake," Maj chided.

"I'm not lying. Why are you, Mother?"

"Svana!" The king straightened, towering over her like the trees.

Maj strode up to the king and took his arm, whispering to him. "I was worried about this, dear. She's been spoiled so much she thinks she can do whatever she wants. And now, when she can't get away with it, she lies and blames someone else."

How could Mother do this? Why was she lying? What did I do wrong? Svana took her father's hand. "Please, Papa."

"Enough!" The king tore his hand from Svana.

Lord Magnar stepped forward. "Please, Your Highness. Svana is young and has always been truthful. Perhaps Svana misunderstood and interpreted your words, my lady, as wishing for the apples from the woods and wanted to surprise you."

"No, that's not what happened," Svana pleaded but Lord Magnar held up his hand to her.

"Look," Maj said to Alric, "even your closest advisor indulges her. If we don't do something now, it will only get worse."

The king patted the queen's hand. "What do you suggest, my love?"

Maj tapped a finger to her chin in thought, then said, "Let her see others don't keep liars for company. Keep her out of your presence until she is willing to tell the truth. Once she sees how ostracizing it is, she will learn that lying takes away those you love and makes you alone."

Not see Papa? Svana shook her head. "No. Please, Papa."

The lords stiffened, glancing at one another.

"Your Highness," Magnar interjected, "that is a bit extreme."

The king held up his hand. "Maj is right." He took a deep breath and sighed. "But complete separation would be impossible. So, it will be limited to meals and events until you are willing to tell the truth in this matter. That is final." King Alric marched across the room and toward the door.

"Your Highness," Lord Magnar said. "If she is to be out of your presence, someone will need to be looking after her. Also, to keep her out of trouble."

Even Lord Magnar believed she was lying. She looked up at him, tugging his tunic, but he only patted her hand.

"I would be willing to volunteer one of my men to this task," Magnar continued.

"No," the king said. "Maj is right. You dote on her."

"My king—" Maj began.

"The hunter then, my king," Magnar interrupted. "He is a good man and has proven faithful in guarding her so far. Game has also been low of late. Perhaps steady work would be a just reward for saving Svana's life."

Alric hesitated, then nodded. "Someone who is not biased towards her but honest and faithful is just what is needed. What do you say, Arvid?"

The hunter bowed. "It would be an honor."

The king turned away and took Maj's arm. Maj's jaw twitched but she followed Alric and left the room.

Svana tugged on Lord Magnar's tunic and shook her head. "Lord Magnar?"

He put a finger to his lips. And winked. Leaning down, he whispered. "You have never lied, my dear princess. I swear I will learn the truth in this matter and bring it to your father. Until then, stay away from the queen. Trust me?"

She threw her arms around his neck and squeezed. Taking a step back, Svana held his hand like ladies at court when knights swear to protect them with their lives. "With all my heart, my lord."

Lord Magnar smiled and bowed. As he walked toward the door, he gestured to the hunter to follow.

Arvid. She should get used to his name.

Sighing, she sat on the couch and swung her legs. The other lords left the room one by one with downcast eyes. Lord Dahl gave a small smile as he passed but without his usual cheer. Svana reached into her pocket.

"Lord Dahl." She pulled out the apple she saved him. "For you."

He smiled as he took it but in a sad way. Like tears would stream through his beard at any moment. "Thank you, my princess."

She settled down on the couch as the last of the lords left. Magnar and Arvid stood in the corner whispering.

"Here." The boy plopped down beside her and handed her an apple as he bit into another.

Taking it, she realized she never did give them to Mother.

"I don't understand this," Magnar whispered to Arvid. "Something doesn't seem right. Being her guard will have its challenges and risks. Are you willing to help us? Protect her from *all* threats that might come to her?"

Arvid nodded. "I swear."

Magnar hesitated. "Even if you have to defy the queen?"

Mother? Why would she be a threat? Dropping the apple, Svana dashed from the room.

Lord Magnar called after her but she didn't stop. Footsteps echoed behind her but as long as they didn't catch up, she didn't care. She ran down corridors and stairs, ignoring their fading calls, until she reached the door to her mother's private garden. Not pausing in her rush, Svana collided with the door and pushed it open. Keeping to the main path, she scanned the rows as she ran.

Everything was green and in bloom, flowers waving in the summer breeze. In the center of the garden, Svana spotted Queen Maj beside a rose bush.

She skidded to a stop before her. "Why did you lie to Father?"

Maj looked down at her, scowling. "You won't just leave it alone, you little pain."

Svana jumped back.

"Always the little princess." Her mother stepped toward her as her brow lowered over her eyes and darkened her face. "Doted on and adored. The people don't even think of me as their queen."

"Mother?" Svana stepped back.

"I am *not* your mother!"

Not my mother?

"I will not be second again. Not to a child!" Maj towered above her like a giant, the breeze blowing her black hair like a raging storm.

A tug on Svana's belt pulled her backwards. The hunter's son, Bjorn, tossed her behind him. He planted his feet and crouched like he was going to spring at the queen.

The breeze settled. Gazing down at the boy, Maj held her chin high. "I'll have to keep an eye on you, won't I?"

"Princess Svana!" Lord Magnar and Arvid entered the garden.

"Here," Maj called. When they approached, she pointed at Svana. "Insolent as ever. Make sure she does not come into my garden again."

"Yes, my lady." Magnar took Svana's hand and led her back to the castle.

Svana didn't fight him, too confused and lost from the journey in the woods then her mother's words. *Not my mother?* Then…who was?

Once inside, Magnar left her alone as he finished talking with Arvid. Bjorn looked at his father and the lord before standing between them and Svana. He removed his knife from his belt and passed it to Svana. "Do you know how to use a knife?"

She shook her head.

"I can teach you. You can hide it in your boot." He paused at the garden door before turning to Svana, smiling. "Don't worry. I'll watch your back."

Chapter 4

BJORN REPLACED THE box's cover and waited until Svana and the bears had disappeared. Picking up the reins, he guided Tindra down the narrow cliff path and across the river. The bears' claws and massive paw prints left a clear trail in the dirt which he followed.

Scanning the forest floor, he searched for Svana, his hands shaking with anticipation of finding her. Was she dead? Something deep in his mind screamed but it couldn't break through the hand upon his mind.

Tindra stopped and stomped her hoof. Kicking the horse's sides, he ordered her forward but she tossed her head and twisted to the side, chomping at the bit. Bjorn dismounted, picked up a rock, and tossed it. Halfway through the air, sparks flared and the rock flew backwards. The air shimmered and reflected pinks and yellows as it settled back into place.

"Ah!" Queen Maj's voice screamed in his head. *"She got through. The barrier must have weakened the spell."*

Bjorn stepped forward.

"Stop. There is nothing you can do." She sighed. He could almost hear her pacing around her mirror. *"Come back. I was not expecting her to find the lords. They may be a problem. We must devise a new strategy."* She chuckled. *"And I have just the bait to motivate her."*

Remounting, Bjorn tugged on the reins, wheeling Tindra around, and headed for Castle Alwilda. With the little control he could muster, one side of his mouth turned up at Svana's escape, the first good thing to happen since this all began.

Svana lay on Magnar's back as he strolled down the forest path, no longer running mad. Eyes closed, breathing deeply, and shivering, the chase through the forest still made her tremble. As she tried to swallow the lump in her throat, a sharp pain radiated from where she nicked herself with the knife and felt the tacky stick of blood trickling down to her collarbone.

A nose nuzzled her arm. Opening her eyes slightly, Svana gazed at a pair of big brown ones round with worry. Even in the face of a bear, she would recognize the kind, concerned face of the man who had always listened when she cried.

She petted his head. "I'm okay, Lord Henrik."

Groaning, Svana lifted her head and looked around, her jaw dropping open as she finally took in her surroundings. They were still in the woods, but not as it was before. Bright, golden sunlight streamed through the leaves as puffs of cotton floated down around them. It was like walking in a snowfall but without the cold.

The trees stopped and the forest opened to a large valley. The grass was so thick and green, Svana almost wanted to jump down and lie in it. But the bears continued to a small, two-story cottage shaded by a willow. The windows and door were trimmed in white and were covered with a budding Morning Glory vine. Around the cottage's base were bushes with pink flowers.

And it was quiet. Only the blowing of the breeze and the grunts of the bears echoed in the valley. Svana dismounted and pulled out her bow. With everything that'd happened, she wasn't taking any chances. Crouching, she crept forward.

"Raarrrr?" The bears growled and mumbled to each other, their voices ringing in the silent valley.

"Keep it down," Svana said. "We don't know who's in there."

Several shook their heads and shrugged to each other. Magnar strode past Svana and pushed open the front door with his large paw. Jerking his head inside, he grunted to the others, who entered. Their bulk and heavy paws created some of the loudest racket she had ever heard as they passed through the doorframe and over wooden floors. Magnar held Svana's gaze for a moment before nodding and entering. Hesitantly, Svana replaced her bow but grabbed the knife from her boot before following.

Inside, the ceiling was twice the height Svana expected from the outside. Daylight streamed through large windows onto the wood floors, coloring them a golden hue. On the far side, a cozy fire burned in a hearth flanked by two chairs intricately carved with images of vines and animals. Wooden columns carved like trees supported the second floor. To the right, a curved staircase with a spiral railing led up. The bears spread out and lay down in various sunlit spots throughout the room and closed their eyes as their tongues lolled out of their heads from a yawn before curling up for naps.

"What is this place?" Svana mumbled. She turned to Magnar. "Do you know?"

Magnar huffed and headed for the stairs, each step creaking and groaning from his bulk. When he reached the top, he looked at her before heading down a corridor and out of sight.

Sighing, Svana followed. Not being able to communicate with him was making it difficult to get clear answers. "I sure hope you know where we are."

At the top, she saw Magnar standing beside an open doorway halfway down the corridor. Inside, she saw a bedroom thick with vines and purple flowers clinging to the ceiling and floors. In the center of the room was a bed with a gauzy canopy draping from its four posts which were carved with swirls that reached toward the ceiling. And on the bed was a sleeping woman. She was dressed in a white gown and had long brown hair down to her waist. A shimmering light seemed to hover in the room but the brightest light seemed to come from an oval mirror to one side of the bed.

Magnar gave Svana a slight push into the room. Somehow, the woman hadn't woken up despite the noise downstairs which still reverberated up here. Svana crept up to the bed and looked down at the woman. Gasping, Svana stumbled back. Except for her brown hair and the slight smile on her lips, she could have been Maj's twin.

Glancing at Magnar, she pointed at the woman. "Who's this?"

To her surprise, instead of Magnar growling and baring his teeth at the woman, he padding over to the mirror and looked back to Svana.

Slowly, Svana approached the mirror. Again, it reminded her of the one Maj loved. Shaking her head, she stepped back.

Magnar came alongside her. He turned from her to the mirror then gave a gentle nod.

Sighing, Svana examined it. Along the edge was writing. A little rhyme. Leaning to the side to see the words better, Svana read, "Mirror, mirror, please recall the darkness of the past, and the fall that took us all."

White light swirled into an oval until it shone so brightly Svana had to cover her eyes and stepped back. With a gentle nudge from behind, Svana stumbled forward into the mirror. Hands out to brace herself, she tripped forward, expecting to feel smooth glass. Instead, the light dimmed and Svana blinked to clear her eyes.

She stood in a valley in late afternoon, a few hours before sunset. The trees were bright orange and red as their leaves fell, blanketing the ground. Turning around, Svana saw the cottage she was just in but the vines encircling it only covered the first floor. The door opened and out ran a younger version of the sleeping woman and…a young Maj.

Svana crouched and looked for her knife but it was gone. The two girls, about Svana's age, ran past her. Like she wasn't there.

"Be home before dark," a woman yelled from the door.

Giggling, Maj and the young woman turned back. "We will." They disappeared down a path into the woods.

An explosion of light came from the cottage with a loud bang, causing Svana to jump. The woman in the door ducked before storming back into the house. "What did you do now?"

She knew magic even then. Not wanting to lose the girls, Svana took off down the path.

They laughed and joked as they ran through the trees. Even Maj smiled and joined in the horseplay. She almost seemed…happy. Svana couldn't remember seeing her like this before.

The path led to a field outside a large, stone wall. Svana knew this place. This was Lord Olin's home. She had visited once years ago but hadn't realized the cottage was so close.

A small group of boys and girls gathered around a hay cart. One of them saw the young women approaching.

"Maj. Sonja. Over here," she called.

They ran up to them and melded into the group.

One of the other girls gasped and took a piece of Maj's dress in her hands. "This is beautiful. Where did you get it?"

Maj grinned and began to chat all about her dress and the material while many of the girls oohed and aahed. Most of the boys also seemed to be enamored with her, unable to look away. As Svana scanned each of the girls and boys, Maj was the most beautiful and held the most attention.

Sonja, though, climbed up into the hay cart and curled into a corner. Separate but still part of the group, she watched the others with a small smile. She seemed shy but enjoyed the camaraderie and company around her.

One boy broke away from the group and wandered over to the hay cart. He was nicely dressed, most likely a servant in the fortress, with fair hair and average build. As he stood by the cart, he couldn't stop fidgeting with his hands, shifting his stance as he kept glancing at Sonja out of the corner of his eye.

Finally, with the reddest cheeks Svana had ever seen, he said, "Hi, Sonja."

Sonja glanced at him. "Hi, Ketill." And turned back to the group.

"Ah," he stammered, struggling to find anything to say. "You look beautiful tonight."

Svana choked on a laugh at his awkward attempt.

Sonja whipped around. "Oh." Now she stammered. "Thank you."

This time, Svana had to place a hand over her mouth as she snorted. These two had no idea what they were doing. But they were so cute… Though no one could see her, Svana still turned around to give them some privacy.

That's when she saw Maj's face. The happy smile was gone. The others still chatted around her, oblivious to what was happening, as Maj glared at Sonja and Ketill. Svana watched as a dim flicker of the same fire she'd seen as a child began to grow in them.

"Ketill!"

Up on the battlements stood Lord Olin. Not the one she knew but a younger version. This must be before he was a lord. With a wave of his arm, Olin gestured for Ketill to come inside.

Returning the wave, Ketill said goodbye to the group. Before he left, he grabbed Sonja's hand and gave it a squeeze before running off.

On the battlements, Olin gazed down at them. The way he looked at Sonja was the same expression as the one Svana had seen on Ketill.

He loved her. How many boys were pinning after this girl?

Sonja bit her nail as her cheeks grew as red as a rose. She'd never looked up to see Olin.

Still standing on the battlements, Olin fidgeted a little, his face dropping before walking away.

Svana sighed. With his position as a future lord, he couldn't very well socialize with commoners. She thought back to when he read to her in the evenings as a child. It was always romantic tales where heroes rescued princesses and fell in love. She'd teased him about it then. Now, she wondered if this was why he chose those stories.

"Sonja." Maj stood on the path, her hands on her hips, any hint of happiness gone. "Time to go."

The sun was low in the sky, changing from yellow to orange and red. Brushing the hay off her skirt, Sonja jumped down and joined her sister. Their friends waved and called good-byes as the girls left but only Sonja acknowledged them.

They walked in silence, the shadows deepening as they followed the path home. Svana carefully watched them.

Sonja was oblivious to everything around her, biting her thumbnail and smiling while trying to suppress a giggle. A shy smile still played on her face, Sonja unaware of Maj's steadily growing anger. Maj followed behind, stomping through the leaves and clenching her hands tighter until it looked like she was going to burst.

When Sonja laughed a third time, Maj stopped.

"What's wrong?" Sonja asked.

Maj shook her head. Pursing her lips, she blinked and her whole body eased, as she smiled. "Nothing. I just forgot something in the village. You go ahead, I'll catch up."

Sonja hesitated. "Are you sure?"

Maj took a deep breath. "Yes."

Taking a few steps, Sonja nodded and continued home.

Maj dropped the smile and whirled around, headed back to the village, Svana following.

She marched down the path and out of the woods and toward the battlements. As Svana reached the tree line, her legs froze. For whatever reason, the memory wouldn't let her go any farther. Maj reached the gate where she leaned against the wall beside a lantern. And waited.

Time seemed to speed up just a bit, the sun setting faster than normal. It was almost dark when Ketill exited the gate with a torch in hand.

Maj stood up and smiled. He started when he saw her. With a slight sway, Maj strode up to him. Svana couldn't hear what she said but watched as her stepmother reached out and stroked Ketill's arm. Shrugging, he stepped away from her. Maj frowned but stayed calm as she talked to him. He took another step back and shook his head. At this point, Maj was clenching her jaw and the fire in her eyes was smoldering.

Beside Svana, Sonja appeared. She stopped beside her and watched the scene. Maj's voice raised a little but she still couldn't make out the words. Ketill shook his head one more time and marched toward the gate. Rage upon her face, Maj lifted her arms. Flashes of green lightning sprang from the sky and surrounded Maj. As she lowered her hands, it blazed toward Ketill. He froze as the lightning consumed him. Then fell to the ground.

"Ketill!" Sonja ran toward them. This time, Svana was able to follow.

Tears in her eyes, Sonja collapsed in the dirt beside Ketill's body. Lifting him into her lap, she shook his shoulders. Sonja kept shaking him and calling his name. Svana closed her eyes and looked away.

"Why, Maj?" Sonja screamed at her sister. "Why would you do this?"

Maj casually stepped up to her. "You could've had anyone. But you steal the one person I wanted."

"What are you talking about? He came to me."

"And why would he want you? Look at you." Maj's face contorted as she looked at her sister in her plain dress now covered in dirt and Ketill's blood. "I am the beautiful one. The gem of this stinking village. What was missing?"

"Maybe a heart!" Sonja screamed, shaking with rage.

Maj screamed as she aimed lightning at Sonja.

Lifting one hand, Sonja blocked it with dazzling white light. Svana jumped back from the magic, almost forgetting she wasn't there. Repositioning herself, Maj growled and shot down more lightning. Using both hands,

Sonja stood and blocked it. The flashing magic glared before breaking off with a burst of light.

"Witches!" Guards gathered on the battlements. Pounding feet and yells grew behind the gate. "Arm yourselves! There are witches at the wall!"

Stopping their battle, the sisters fled back toward the woods and disappeared among the trees. Svana had to sprint to keep up with them. They ran for home, occasionally turning back to see if they were followed.

As they reached the valley, Sonja ran ahead of Maj. Gasping for breath, Maj stopped. She watched her sister before picking up a thorn, surrounded it in green mist, and sent it flying toward Sonja.

It landed in the back of Sonja's neck, causing her to stumble. She swallowed and swayed, taking awkward steps before her eyes rolled into her head and fell to the ground.

"Sonja? Maj?" Their parents ran out of the house to the girls.

Their father turned Sonja over and put his ear to her mouth. "She's breathing." Picking up the thorn, he held it out to Maj. "What did you do?"

Maj jutted out her chin.

"Maj?"

Maj crossed her arms and walked several paces away.

With a twist of his hand, her father pulled blue light from Sonja's head with snippets of memory. The images flowed into his mind and in seconds, he had seen it all. Svana stood by and watched, eyes growing wide at the display.

He turned to Maj, shaking his head as he struggled for words. "How could you do this?" He sounded breathless and his voice cracked. "Attack your sister? Kill an innocent boy?"

"He wasn't innocent!" Maj fired back. "He rejected me. She…she knew I liked him. And she took him from me."

"Love cannot be forced or stolen. He did nothing wrong."

"She took everything! Why shouldn't I use everything I have? There was nothing to lose."

He looked down again at Sonja before turning back to Maj. "You know the price of using that kind of magic. Do you know what this will do to you?"

Maj tossed up her hands. "I don't see any price yet. Maybe you just made it up to scare me. Make me act the way you wanted." She lifted her chin. "Maybe there isn't a price for using one type of magic over another."

He shook his head. "I thought I taught you better than that. You are lucky you are too weak to create a lethal dose."

Maj growled as her face darkened. "I am not weak." She lifted her hands, lightning dancing between her hands.

As she brought them down, their father clapped his hands together before pulling them slowly apart. The lightning slammed into a shimmering, transparent barrier and flared off the shield. As he opened his hands wider, the barrier grew around Sonja and her parents. As it reached Maj, she was pushed back.

"What are you doing?!" she screamed.

"Protecting this family."

"No!" Maj pounded on the wall, sending up flashes of light as it pushed her back. When it reached the path to the village, it slowed to a stop. Maj continued to slam her fists against the barrier, yelling and grinding her teeth.

Her father approached her. "Give up this dark magic. And we can talk about how to move forward."

Maj clamped her mouth shut. Standing a little straighter, she raised her chin. "No." She ran into the woods and was gone.

"Maj!" he yelled after her. He waited but she didn't return.

"That was the last time I saw my sister."

Svana spun around. Sonja stood behind her but as she looked in the cottage. And much more awake. To Svana's right, Sonja's parents crouched over her unconscious, younger self.

"My parents did all they could but they couldn't break Maj's curse. They were able to adjust it so the spell merely made me sleep instead of killing me."

"Where are they now?" Svana asked.

"Dead. The magic that supports the barrier is connected to the cottage so I am able to maintain it."

Svana bit her lip and tilted her head to the side.

"Enchantments end either when the caster removes them, certain requirements are met, or the caster dies. When we received no word of Maj or strange, dark magic happening, we hoped she had changed. Then, the bear lords began arriving. One by one. I realized then something had caused my sister to lash out after all this time."

Svana shook her head. "How did you know they were lords?"

Sonja leaned toward her. "Magic users can identify magic and can find their way through it even if they can't dispel it. They let me see who they truly were under all that fur. Unfortunately for Lord Olin"—her cheeks flushed—"there isn't much you can hide when you allow a sorceress to see who you truly are. Don't tell him, okay?"

Svana glanced to where Maj had run. "Why couldn't she enter?"

"This barrier blocks enchantments and people with evil intent. You will be safe as long as you're here. Maj's magic weakens in here but does not end."

Feeling the nick on her neck, Svana thought about the ties and how they loosened for just a moment. "I have a friend who's under her control."

Sonja shook her head. "He cannot enter. Even though it is Maj controlling him, his purpose is for destruction."

Night had fallen in the memory, black with just the glow from the cottage providing light. Sonja's parents carried her inside.

"He said something about a price?"

Sighing, Sonja hung her head. "It is the price of all magic. He only ever told us in a riddle. 'The beauty of magic reflects the heart upon the caster.'"

"What does that mean?"

Sonja shifted. "Please don't ask me anymore. What I told you can stop her. But I'm afraid it will lead to her death."

Death? "Is that the only way?"

"If she is unwilling to change." Sonja wiped a tear from her eye.

Clenching and unclenching her hands, Svana nodded.

"Besides," Sonja went on, "if she continues, it will only be a matter of time."

"Until what?"

Sonja sighed. "Until she destroys herself."

"And how many more will die before that happens?" Svana snapped.

"I am sorry." Sonja gestured to the right. A swirling oval of white light formed. "You are welcome to stay at the cottage as long as you like. I hope you find what you need. If you wish to speak to me again, come back to the mirror."

Walking across the grass, Svana stepped through the oval and into the room with Sonja's sleeping form. The mirror behind her returned to normal. Through the window, Svana could see night had fallen outside.

Magnar lay on a rug watching the mirror and stood when she came through. Absentmindedly, Svana began petting his head, finding it hard not to treat him like an animal in his current form. On the other side of the bed, another bear sat beside it, his head lying beside Sonja. As he sighed, Svana could see Lord Olin in him.

"I don't know what to do, Magnar." Svana sighed. "I understand more now, but she wasn't much help on what to do next." She looked into his big, brown eyes. "Any ideas?" It felt like talking to a dog. But unlike a dog, he could answer her, in a way.

Turning around, Magnar headed out the door and back into the corridor. She followed him to another room. It was another bedroom with only a bed, table, and a lit candle for furnishings.

Placing her bow and arrows in the corner, Svana sat on the bed. "At least no one is sleeping in this one."

Magnar grunted, not appreciating the joke. A moment later, Lord Olin came into the room. In his mouth was a book which he carried over to her.

Taking it from him, Svana read the cover and chuckled. A romance.

"Thank you." She ruffled his head. As they left, she leaned back on the covers, wrapping her arms around the book. Her mind was blank. There seemed so much to think about that she couldn't think of anything. Rolling over, she traced the cover of the book and thought back to Bjorn's surprise just a few years after meeting him.

"Svana!"

"AH!" Svana jumped and dropped the book she'd been reading.

Bjorn leaned over the back of her chair, chuckling with a big grin spread across his face. Swinging her book, Svana attempted to knock him in the head but he shielded himself with his arm. "Don't scare me like that."

"Come on." He hopped backward, waving for her to follow. "I want to show you something."

Svana knelt in her chair and glanced about her personal sitting room. "Where's your father?"

Bjorn huffed. "I told him I would watch you for a while. Now come on."

In the last three years she knew Bjorn, this was the giddiest she had ever seen him. Usually, he was serious. Straight faced. Steady. Calculating. Boring. Except when he was teaching her to wield a knife or to fight and she got to flip him over her shoulder. But this was different. Tossing her book on the chair, she ran after him.

Bjorn set the chase, running ahead then waiting for her at a corner before dodging left or right before she could catch up. She was gasping for breath when he led her to an area primarily used by servants, well out of the way of the main living quarters. To the left was a stairwell leading down to the servant quarters, kitchens, and other rooms for various tasks. As Svana headed for these, Bjorn dodged to the right and up a darkened staircase.

Svana hesitated. Slowly creeping forward, she craned her neck to see up the stairs. They had always been dark. As long as she could remember. That wing had never been in use or lit in any way. It was so dark Svana often forget it was there, feeling the shadows creating a wall she would not, could not, cross. Halfway up, Bjorn waved to her again. Swallowing, Svana hiked up her skirts and headed up the dim steps.

At the top was a corridor with doors leading off into various rooms. Not a single tapestry or portrait adorned the walls. The light from the windows was filtered through layers of dirt. Cobwebs hung from the ceiling and corners like little traps reaching out to catch Svana. Dust covered every inch and great clouds welled up as they passed.

Coughing, Svana called, "Where are we going?"

"Almost there," Bjorn yelled back down the corridor.

Svana ran to where he waited by an open door, grinning from ear to ear. "Now, what is so important?"

"Inside." He jerked his head toward the room.

Sighing, Svana walked through the doorway. It had once been sleeping quarters, now covered in dust and cobwebs. Squinting to see in the semi-dark, she could make out the shapes of a bed, vanity, and table and chairs covered with white cloths. To the right was a large fireplace with another cloth hanging over what was probably a portrait. With a lazy turn, Svana shrugged toward Bjorn.

Still wearing a big grin, Bjorn took her hand and led her to the fireplace as she rolled her eyes. Taking her shoulders, he stood her before the fireplace then went to the edge of the cloth. He gave it a single tug and it fell down.

It was a painting of a beautiful woman whose skin was white and smooth except for the smile lines around her mouth which made her seem to glow. Long, golden hair hung past her shoulders to her waist where it pooled on her chair. She wore a rich, red gown with gold cording on the sleeves and bodice. Bright green eyes shone from the portrait, like the woman was truly there and not just a painting.

Svana stepped back. Reaching up, she took a bit of her own hair and twirled it around her finger. *Could it be?* Ever since she learned Maj wasn't her mother, she'd wondered who was. *Is this her?*

Bjorn stood next to her and gazed at the portrait. "I thought she looked like you, too." He turned to Svana with that goofy grin.

Jumping up, Svana wrapped her arms around Bjorn and hugged him tight. He squeezed her back. When she let go, she gazed at the portrait, studying every line, every shade of color so she would never forget her mother's face.

Svana strode down the corridor, the bright, spring sun shining through the windows. She tried not to skip as she took in the beautiful day. Turning a corner, she saw Bjorn leaning against the wall.

Oh great.

"Afternoon, Bjorn," she said and walked past.

Pushing off the wall, Bjorn followed, shaking his head at her perky demeanor. "Where are you headed?"

Images of her mother's leather-bound journal, tucked safely in a vanity drawer, came to mind. "I'm going to do a little reading. So you don't need to follow me."

Bjorn sighed. "Nice try. I know what 'a little reading' is."

Scowling, Svana could still feel him hovering when she found the journal and had curled up under her mother's portrait while reading it. She remembered him fussing over her during the winter months, wrapping her in blankets because she refused to start a fire, afraid someone would see the smoke. Pushing her out of the room when he thought it was enough. If it hadn't been for him, she probably would've gotten frostbite or pneumonia during those cold winter months.

"Sometimes I regret showing you."

"Why?" Svana whirled around.

"Because I don't want you to get hurt." He took a step back. Biting his lip, he glanced out a window. "Because, if anything happens, I wouldn't forgive myself."

"Because it is your duty to protect me."

"Because you're…my friend."

Svana bit her tongue. "I can only go when no one will miss me. Today, Father has gone hunting and Maj is busy with some cleaning project so I have all day. Who knows when my next chance will be?" Playing with her fingers, she looked down. "Do you know I still don't know her name?"

"Not even a hint?"

"No. She never used it in the journal and nothing is monogrammed." She shook her head. "And I can't ask anyone in case Maj hears. This is the only way I can learn anything about her."

Sighing, Bjorn stood his ground for a moment then stepped up to her. "I'll help you look."

Smiling, they walked down the corridor side by side. Rounding another corner, Svana smelled a whiff of a wood fire. It wasn't the kind from a hearth but a large, blazing one. Like the bonfires during festival days. As they neared a window, she glanced outside.

On the grounds below, her stepmother ordered servants carrying old furniture to a fire consuming tables, chairs, boxes, and trunks. Sitting on the grass waiting to be added to the flames was an old vanity covered with dust and pieces of a four-poster bed. Examining each item, Svana's heart beat faster as her throat clogged.

She barreled down the corridor.

"Svana?" Bjorn called.

Ignoring him, she raced down the stairwell to a door leading outside and shoved it open. The smell of smoke choked her as she ran toward the fire.

"No! Stop!"

The heat blasted against her skin as she reached the blaze. A servant emptied a trunk into the fire, tossing gowns and cloaks atop the furniture. The flames lowered then sprang higher as it ate through the clothing from the edges to their center, disintegrating everything into ash and soot.

"That's my mother's!"

With her hand outstretched toward the fire, she was stopped by an arm around her waist. Bjorn tightened his grip and heaved her off her feet, dragging her backwards.

"No!"

She thrashed, kicking and clawing at his arms and head. He carried her a few feet and set her down as she slipped around in his grasp.

A servant carried her mother's portrait. She elbowed Bjorn in the gut and slammed her head back into his nose. As he doubled over, she ran toward the servant. Just as she reached him, he threw the portrait into the flames.

"Mother!"

The fire grew around the wood frame. The paint bubbled across the queen's face, disfiguring and discoloring the image. The edges cracked and curled in. A flame burnt through the center and reached her face.

"Mother!" Pushing the servant aside, Svana reached into the fire.

Again, arms clasped her around her waist, tearing her away. Bjorn's arms pinned hers to her sides as he dragged her back from the scorching heat.

"Control your charge or you'll be excused." Maj stood over them.

Svana gritted her teeth. Growling, she tried to spring at the queen but Bjorn held her tight. Picking her up off the ground, he dragged her away from the scene as the fire grew with more of her mother's things.

Inside, Bjorn kicked the door shut and placed himself in front of it before setting Svana down, keeping a firm grip on her arms.

Taking a swing at him, Svana struggled. "Let go. They are burning my mother!"

But he held tighter to her wrists. She kicked and pummeled him as best she could with him holding her back. Then the tears came. The hits slowed. Choking, she swung once more.

"I hate you. Get out of my way. I hate you."

Loosening his grip, he waited for her to take another swing. When she didn't, he held up his hands. Reaching into his tunic, he pulled out a leather-bound book and gave it to her. Running her hand against the cover, Svana opened it and saw her mother's handwriting.

"It was all I could grab."

Wrapping her arms around it, Svana wept. She didn't care who heard. Falling forward, she buried her face in Bjorn's neck and held him as the tears wracked her body.

Chapter 5

SVANA GASPED AND opened her eyes. The room was dark except for the silver glow of the full moon shining through the window.

Wide awake, Svana sat up in bed and looked about the empty room, her eye catching the yellow light under the door. Tossing the blankets aside, she got up and creaked the door open. The light was coming from Sonja's room. She could also hear the bears' grunts coming from that direction. Grabbing her bow and quiver, she snuck down the corridor.

All seven bears were inside Sonja's room. Lord Olin sat with his head lying beside her, occasionally sniffing as he watched her sleep. Lord Magnar sat next to him, growling something. Whatever he said made Lord Dane roll his eyes from where he lay behind them. In the corner, Lord Dahl seemed to have found a honey pot and was licking it clean while Lord Vidar pawed at his head, trying to pull the older lord's head out of it. She bit back a smile as she thought he most likely wanted some too. Lords Henrik and Axel were curled up on rugs fast asleep.

It was almost a normal night. Except for the enchanted woman, the bear lords, and visiting a cottage protected by magic. And Maj hunting them down. *What have I gotten us all into?* Sighing, Svana turned away from the door and tiptoed downstairs.

All was quiet and dark. The fire still burned in the hearth, giving it a warm, cozy feel. Svana wandered into the kitchen and peeked into the cupboards. Surprisingly, they were full with fresh food. Svana shuffled around dried meats, breads, and sweets, all comforting or hearty. Perhaps it was the magic also providing what she needed.

Closing the cupboards, Svana strode to the fire and sat in one of the plush chairs. The warm hearth eased the aches in her joints, pain she hadn't even realized was there before. She hadn't relaxed since…she didn't remember when. Yet, she felt restless. Gathering her golden hair in her hands, she packed it behind her head, holding it off her neck as she stared into the waving flames.

We can't keep going like this. All she'd been doing was running scared. And she was tired of it.

Knock, knock, knock.

Dropping her hair, Svana turned toward the door. With a quick glance up the stairs to see if the lords had heard, she hesitantly walked toward the entrance.

The thumping came again. It didn't sound like a fist but like wood striking wood. She glanced through the small window set in the door. A hand-held mirror with green mist snaking around the frame hovered outside. Within the mirror was the scowling image of Maj.

"Open the door, dear," she said.

Svana flattened herself against the wall. *How is she here?*

"Be a good girl and open the door."

Clamping her mouth shut, Svana took her bow and strung an arrow. Grabbing the handle, she swung the door open and lifted her bow, aiming at the glass.

"Is that any way to greet your mother?"

"You are not my mother."

"But I was the only one you knew."

The mirror flew inside and darted about the house, examining every corner of the place.

"What do you want? Sonja said you couldn't get in here."

"And I'm not here. Only things with intent to harm can't get in and I can't harm you through this mirror." It floated back toward Svana and settled in front of her. "Stop that scowl. You'll get wrinkles."

"What do you want?" Svana spoke slowly through gritted teeth.

"I thought it was time to end this. I'm tired of chasing you. So, I bring a proposal. It is out by the barrier."

Svana huffed. "I'm not going anywhere with you."

"You stubborn mule. You'll be safe. I can't reach you. But if you want to keep running, fine. But how far do you think you'll get? Who will help you? And how long do you think you can run with those bears before one of them gets hurt? If you would like this to be over, like I do, then come with me." The mirror swerved around her and out the door.

Svana's hand tightened on her bow until it shook. How long until one of the lords was hurt? She wanted to say she would protect them but knew the truth. They would jump in front of the danger before she had a chance to react.

"Coming?"

Replacing the arrow, Svana marched to the door and out.

The moon lit the ground and trees, bathing the valley in silver. The mirror floated ahead, leading back down the path she and the bears entered from. They traveled the path in silence. Coming to the edge of the barrier, Svana saw Bjorn standing on the other side, Tindra with him.

"Bjorn?" Svana stopped a foot away.

His face was expressionless.

"He won't answer, child," Maj said. "Now, come back to the castle or"—she waved her hand toward Bjorn who reached behind him and removed a knife—"I will have to hurt him."

He laid the blade across his wrist.

"No!" Svana ran to the edge of the barrier but stopped short of crossing. "That's your idea of a deal?"

"I would rather not fight. Threatening him seemed the best course. Your answer?"

Bjorn pushed and a drop of blood slipped around his wrist and fell to the ground.

"Monster!" Svana jumped across the barrier. Pulling the knife from her boot, she lunged at Bjorn. As she hoped, he used his own knife to block hers. Swinging around, Svana swiped downward. Measuring her strikes, she wanted to keep him active, not hurt him. But that was difficult when he struck without the same restraint.

With a twist to the right, Bjorn caught her knife. Their blades crossed, struggling against each other. Svana looking into his face, only inches from hers. His eyes were blank and emotionless, not even heated from the fight. But there was something, a little spark in the back that looked like…fear.

Spinning her back into his chest, Svana grabbed his wrist. Ducking, she buckled his leg with a push from her hip and pulled him over her shoulder before dropping him onto his back. Bjorn gasped as he hit the ground. Winded, it would take him a second to recover. Using his arm as leverage, she rolled him over and sat on him, pinning him to the ground.

"Keep fighting, dear." Maj's voice came from the other side of the barrier, cool and bored. "But as long as I have control of him, there is nothing you can do."

Bjorn tossed dirt toward her with his free hand. As she ducked, her grip loosened and he rolled to his knees. Knuckles white, he clenched the hilt of his knife as he stood before her.

"I can have him use this anytime I want." The mirror floated between them. Maj gripped her wrist with a hiss. Clenching her teeth, her eyes narrowed at Svana. "Well, what is your choice? Come home and settle this, or watch your childhood friend die."

Svana glanced at Bjorn. His wrist still bled but he did nothing to stop it. He was completely at her stepmother's mercy, unable to think or act for himself. Maj was right. This had to end. And there was only one way to stop it.

Squeezing the hilt of her knife, her hands shook before throwing it to the side.

"Good girl." The mirror pivoted. "Bjorn."

Rising, Bjorn walked around behind her. Svana's hands shook as she fought the urge to defend herself. She'd surrendered. When she heard the *swish*, she blinked in recognition before the hilt of his knife smacked the left side of her skull and she blacked out.

As Svana dropped to the ground, Bjorn reached out and caught her, holding her limp in his arms.

"Bring her back here," Maj said. "I'll take care of her personally."

The mirror went dark as the green mist dispersed. Bjorn caught it with one hand as it dropped from where it was hovering.

Eyes closed, Svana breathed evenly, like she was asleep. Loose strands of her golden hair clung to her face and drifted across his arm. With a shaking hand, Bjorn reached over and brushed them away.

Tucking her in closer with his left hand, Bjorn wrapped his right arm under her knees as he lifted her up and carried her to Tindra. He dropped the mirror in a saddlebag then lifted Svana onto the horse's back before swinging up behind her.

"Grrraaa." A low, rumbling growl grew behind him.

A bear stood within the barrier. One she'd been with at the river. The animal crouched, muscles tensing under his thick fur. His snout wrinkled as he bared his long, white teeth.

Bjorn gazed back at him. He couldn't move. Couldn't convey what he wanted. Clenching his jaw, he hoped somehow the bear would understand. *Help me.*

The bear blinked. As the growl eased, his lips lowered as he lifted his head.

Forcing his taut muscles to move, Bjorn nodded, turning Tindra about. The horse raced off away from the barrier and toward Castle Alwilda.

Chapter 6

HEAD THROBBING, SVANA awoke. The trees seemed to split and double as she looked at them, coming in and out of focus. Tindra's gait didn't help as she rocked back and forth. Closing her eyes, she leaned forward, thinking she was going to hurl. Bjorn's stiff arm around her waist kept her steady as she slid to the side.

As the queasiness passed, she looked up at him. "Beautiful day we're having," she mumbled.

Nothing. *A roll of the eye? A shake of the head? Something?* He was there but wasn't. Maj's enchantment had him completely shut in. Even if she did what the queen wanted, was there any way to help him?

She took in the forest around them. As they passed trees and gullies, she recognized them more and more. They were the same ones she'd met Bjorn in. Almost died in.

They rode in silence. Soon, the trees thinned and Castle Alwilda loomed ahead as they made their way to the gates. Svana gripped the saddle horn. Once inside, she'd never come out. *I'm riding to my death.*

A fine layer of green mist edged the doors as the wooden gates swung open. They rode inside. The gate swung closed with a *clunk* behind them. Svana felt Bjorn flinch.

They came to the stable yard beside the barn and Bjorn dropped to the ground. Svana swung her leg over to dismount when Bjorn stepped in front of her. Grabbing her waist, he lowered her down before taking her elbow and hauling her toward the castle.

Halfway, he halted. His grip tightened as his hand shook. Veins in his neck popped as the muscles in his jaw twitched.

He doesn't want this but he can't fight. Reaching her free hand around, Svana placed hers over his and squeezed. When she let go, she took a step forward and Bjorn moved with her.

The large double doors clacked and groaned as they opened to the great hall. Swallowing, Svana lifted her chin as they entered. *If I'm going to die, I won't be cowering.*

Torches burned in sconces, crackling and flickering as Svana and Bjorn made their way to the dais. Maj stood before a mirror. She gazed into it, her brow furrowed as she inspected her arms and neck. They walked to the base of the dais and stopped.

Through the mirror, Maj glared them. "So, the little princess returns." Twirling about, she strode down from the dais.

Svana took a step forward but Bjorn held her in place. "Well? You said you wanted to finish this."

Shaking her head, Maj puckered her lips. Dragging a hand across Svana's hair, Maj brushed back the dirt-encrusted, oily strands from where they stuck to her face. "My, my, look who's acting like a queen." Her nails dug into Svana's golden locks as she gripped a fistful. "It feels great, doesn't it? Thinking you have the power."

"What power?"

"Don't act like a fool. I know she told you. 'The beauty of magic reflects the heart upon the caster.' You really think you can use that against me?"

With a flick of her hand, Maj tossed Svana away before wrapping a hand around her wrist. "Well, you already have, haven't you? Mother and father adored her. The talented sorceress. I didn't mind that she was better at magic. I had something else. Beauty. I was fawned over and boys flocked to me." Her brow lowered. "Except one. The only one that mattered. Instead, she had to go and take him too. So I took him back."

As Maj spoke, Svana thought of the memories she'd seen at Sonja's.

Maj growled. "Then they shunned me. Thought I would come crawling back, begging for forgiveness when I couldn't make it on my own. But I found a way without them. I married a king. Praised and lauded over… At least when I didn't have a little brat hanging from my skirt. Then you grew up. And the people praised you. Even your father chose you over me."

Storming up the dais's steps, Maj returned to the mirror and rubbed her palm against the frame. "Mirror,

mirror, reflect the time, of the day being the fairest was no longer mine."

Green mist swirled within the glass like a raging thundercloud. Stepping through, Maj disappeared. Bjorn dragged Svana to the mirror. With a shove, he tossed her through before following. Green engulfed her before fading to a cliff top. Pine trees rose up behind a small camp. Rounding the tent, Svana saw a small hunting party. Sitting outside the tent was Maj with Lord Vidar standing behind her, chatting to Bjorn, who nodded. By the look of his tight smile, he was being polite. Maj, on the other hand, closed her eyes and rubbed her temples. To the left, standing beside the cliff, was Svana and her father stroking falcons perched on their arms.

She remembered this day. It was only a few months back. The next day Lord Vidar was sent away like the other lords and she had no one.

The real Maj stood behind the king, scowling at them like she could burn them both with her gaze. Svana slowly walked forward.

"This is when it changed," Maj said.

King Alric brushed his falcon's feathers as it chirped. As he did, he glanced at Svana. "You look lovely, dear."

The memory Svana jumped. She'd been surprised to hear him speak to her. When was the last time he'd given her a compliment?

Memory-Svana's mouth gaped before she said, "Thank you."

Ten years. They hadn't said anything personal to each other in ten years. So much had changed. She wasn't a

little girl anymore. But, him seeing her, talking to her…
it'd felt like she had a father again.

King Alric chuckled. The memory continued. He said
something more but she couldn't hear it. But this wasn't
her memory.

Glancing towards the memory Maj, she watched as her
stepmother's face darkened, her hair shading her face as
her eyes smoldered with that furious fire. Now, it seemed
to consume her.

"He had been so faithful," Maj said, turning back
once more to the king. "He was all mine but then I lost
him. My beauty wasn't enough anymore. And I knew
something had to be done."

Waving her arm, the green oval appeared and Maj led
them through. Bjorn grabbed Svana again and pushed
her back into the great hall. She felt like she was being
swallowed by a storm as the mist surrounded her. As it
faded, she caught sight of Maj marching toward a bowl
beside her throne.

"Why is beauty so important to you?" Svana
screamed at her.

"Because it is all I have!" Maj pulled back her sleeve.
"And now…" The skin was withered, wrinkled like a
blanket on uneven ground, and thin to almost translucent.
When she revealed her neck, deep lined wrinkles like tree's
bark reached up toward her face. "I don't even have that."

Clamping her mouth shut, Maj's chin trembled as a
tear slid down her cheek. "Do you know why Alric married
me? I do. Not for love. But so his daughter had a mother.
That is all he cared about." She brushed the back of her
fingers against her check. "But he did admire my beauty."

Snapping her eyes shut, she shook her head. "His love didn't matter to me. I was a queen. The people loved me." A growl rumbled in her throat. "Then you grew up. And the people thought of *their* queen. Admired her. I was nothing to them." Maj whirled toward Svana, grinding her teeth in frustration. "Even now, the mess you are, they would admire you. So I did what I needed to keep what I had. And now"—Maj reached into the bowl and picked up a red apple—"we are back at the beginning." She held it up by her fingertips and brought it to Svana. "Remember when I sent you for apples, dear?"

"When you tried to kill me?"

Maj held out the apple to Svana. "Let's end it."

Svana glanced from the apple to Maj. "You want me to eat that when I know it's going to kill me? Give me a reason."

"For the same reason you came back." She turned to Bjorn and held out the apple. "Maybe he'd like it."

As his hand raised, Svana grasped his wrist. "No!"

Maj held up the apple again. "Eat and he lives."

Svana looked at the blood red apple. "What guarantee do I have that you will keep your promise?"

"If you don't eat this now, nothing is left to keep me from killing him. But, if you do, at least you did all you could to save him." She held the apple closer to her. "Do we have a deal?"

Svana felt Bjorn tug on her elbow, like he was trying to pull her back. But there wasn't much of a choice.

Wrapping her arms around Bjorn's neck, she hugged him. "Find a way to stop her," she whispered. She pushed Bjorn away and took the apple from Maj.

She could see her reflection in the fruit, tangled hair and covered in dirt. As Svana raised it to her mouth, a hand clamped on her wrist. Bjorn pushed against her arm, straining against her.

"What are you doing?" Maj roared. Raising her hand, green mist swirled around it.

Bang! The great hall's wooden doors flew open. Magnar and the other lords leapt inside. "Raaarrrrrrr!"

Maj growled and waved her hands, green mist slithering across the floor. Guards rushed into the room from side doors and leveled spears at the lords.

"No!" Svana grasped Bjorn's hand and tried to pry it off. "Bjorn, let go!" Svana tried to push him with her shoulder but he was as solid as a brick wall.

Several of the lords sprang into action, roaring at the guards, chomping at the spears, or rearing up on their hind legs, towering over them. Two ran down the length of the hall toward Maj, Svana, and Bjorn.

Raising her hands, Maj gathered more green mist but was knocked from her feet by Lord Dane, his eyes spinning with rage. Maj pushed her hand toward his eyes, and the mist converged on him. Dane threw his head back and roared, waving back and forth as he tried to shake it off. The mist sank into his eyes, taking on a green glow.

Lord Magnar growled at him but Dane braced his legs. Mouth hanging open, Dane challenged Magnar, pouncing up and down on his front paws as he bared his teeth.

Maj slowly got to her knees, arms shaking with the effort. Her hair was disheveled and half white. The wrinkles had climbed to her cheeks. As her eyes glowed with a burning, red fire, she turned to Svana and Bjorn. Thrusting her arms forward, she sent a wave of green over Bjorn.

He doubled over in a cough as the green mist, thick as fog, hung around him. The grip on Svana's arms loosened. Wrapping his arm around hers, he placed her back against his chest, clamping her arms to her sides and the apple away from her mouth. But he couldn't stand, collapsing to his knees as he wheezed for air.

"Bjorn!" Svana screamed as he pulled her down.

He twisted her wrist and the apple flew from her hand.

Bjorn gasped. The green around him faded. As he blinked, the cold, unseeing edge to his eyes faded.

Maj screamed. Falling to the stone floor, she doubled over, withering in pain. Lines crawled up her neck and across her face. Like water flowing through cracks in stone, the wrinkles reached her hair which turned from black to pure white.

Svana gazed at her stepmother, horrified at the transformation. Taking a step forward, Svana was pushed back by a paw…hand?

"Stay away from her, Princess."

Lord Magnar? Glancing over her shoulder, she saw the lord still looking very much like a bear but shrinking and shedding his fur.

"Aaaahhhhh!" The screech resounded throughout the hall. Maj had withered till she was a mass of wrinkles. She reached out a trembling hand, and green smoke swirled but floated listlessly to the floor. As she continued to pour out green mist, her skin wrinkled and peeled back, blackening on the edges. Smoke began to waft from Maj's shriveled form.

Pushing past Magnar, Svana dropped to her knees beside her stepmother as she wheezed. The deep wrinkles were black and glowed lightly orange like embers. "Maj, stop. You can't do this anymore."

Maj's wheezing became gasps with a resounding growl. "I won't be second again. You will come with me to the grave." Maj thrust a burning hand toward Svana's face.

Pulled up by her belt, Svana stumbled into Bjorn.

With an echoing cry, Maj curled in on herself and crumbled to ash.

With shaky breaths, Svana stared at the ground and the grey dust in the shape of the queen's form. "She's gone."

The hall fell silent. Guards held their heads, no longer battling the lord bears.

Lord Magnar, once again a man in his lord's livery, stood behind her. The other lords approached, human as well, and looked at the spot Maj had fallen.

Setting his jaw, Magnar said, "The beauty inside reflected on the outside."

Bjorn's arms tightened around Svana's shoulders. She grasped his arms and sighed. When she glanced at Magnar, Svana scrunched her forehead. The lord was looking at her with a raised brow. No. He was looking past her. *He's looking at Bjorn.* But why was Magnar looking at him so funny?

Out of the corner of her eye, Svana saw Lord Dahl walk over to the apple and pick it up. Dusting it off, he raised it to his lips.

"Lord Dahl!"

Jumping, the lord fumbled with the apple. "What? Her magic is gone now, yes? Shouldn't let this go to waste. Symmetrical, fits perfectly into the hand, the red shading not too light or too dark. Just right." He raised it to his mouth.

"And she may have used poison instead of magic."

Thinking about this for a moment, Lord Dahl dropped it.

"A wise point, Your Highness."

Svana chuckled at the old, teasing nickname. But when she turned to him, her smile faded. Placing a hand on his chest, Lord Magnar sank to his knee and lowered his head. In turn, each lord bowed, creating a circle around her. With a squeeze to her shoulder, Bjorn stepped back. Svana's jaw dropped as she watched him take a knee and bow his head.

What?

Chapter 7

LEANING AGAINST A parapet, Svana looked upon the village below as a breeze blew her silver skirt and loose golden hair. Even with the setting sun, she could see the people as they closed their doors, giddy and excited as they made their way to the castle. The festival grounds were dotted with remains of the games from the afternoon's celebration of her coronation. If only she'd felt as excited. Returning to her mother's open journal, she read the entry.

I am pregnant. I can't describe how excited I am to have my first child. As I'm sitting here in the garden, there are swans swimming in the pond. White feathers, black and orange beaks. Their grace and beauty as they swim make me hope I have a child who is just as beautiful as they are. So, if it is a girl, I will name her Svana, after the swan.

Closing the journal, Svana turned her face into the wind, letting the gentle breeze blow around her. It was calming. Lifted and stilled her trembling heart.

To her left in the garden below, she spotted Lord Olin and Sonja strolling through the rose patch. Sonja's arm was wrapped around his elbow as he rested his hand over hers. Mostly they just walked in silence, peaceful smiles on their faces. Lord Olin pointed something out and started talking. And kept talking. The longer he went on, the more flustered he became, waving his hands in dramatic gestures, his face falling, and talked faster as his face turned red. But Sonja smiled, reached up, and gently kissed his cheek. He quieted and they continued their walk as they rested their heads against each other.

Svana leaned her head on her hand and smiled.

"What?" Bjorn stepped up beside her and leaned over the parapet.

"Just Sonja and Lord Olin."

Bjorn clenched his jaw and straightened. "Does it bother you how much she looks like Maj?"

She thought for a moment then shook her head. "No. I actually feel bad she lost Maj. She'd really hoped her sister would change." She watched as the two rounded a corner and disappeared behind a tree. "But at least she came back to a love like that. Can you imagine what caring for someone that much would be like?"

Bjorn cleared his throat and looked out over the village and fields.

Svana chuckled. *I guess love talk makes boys uncomfortable.*

After a while he started fidgeting. First, he glanced at her out of the corner of his eye, then ran his fingers through his hair before clearing his throat. But he didn't say anything.

"What?"

Tugging at his tunic's collar, Bjorn glanced at her before examining the parapet.

Are his cheeks turning red? Svana smirked as she tried not to laugh. The last time she saw someone like this was when… Slowly, her smile dropped and her eyes widened. The last time was when Ketill made his feelings known to Sonja.

"You look beautiful," Bjorn whispered.

Now it was Svana's turn to blush. She picked at her silver gown and pulled the grey fur cloak weighing down her shoulders close. Scratching her head, she was careful not to disturb the flowers woven into the braids wrapped around her head like a crown.

Bjorn cleared his throat. "Perhaps that is too familiar with a queen."

"It's fine," Svana said but then bit her lip. "I'm not sure I'm ready to be queen."

Bjorn straightened up. "But you were born to it."

"I know, but I never really thought about what that meant. Besides, Father never taught me how to rule."

Bjorn hesitantly tucked a loose strand of golden hair behind her ear. "I think you will be a good queen. Besides, Lord Magnar and the others are here. They'll help you. They've been like fathers to you for as long as I can remember."

A smile tugged at her lips. "They have been." She swallowed, trying to clear the crack in her voice. "They're more like fathers to me than mine ever was."

"But I believe he loved you."

Svana shuffled her feet. "I'm not so sure."

Bjorn leaned toward her. "I do. That memory Maj showed us. He still cared. Wanted to find a way to reconnect with you. He just didn't get a chance."

Blinking, a tear slid down her cheek. Sniffing, she looked up to him and smiled. "Thank you." Biting her lip, she went on. "For everything. I wouldn't be here if it wasn't for you."

Bjorn hesitated. Breathing deep, he said, "And I'll continue to be here. I don't have much to give but what I can I will."

As he shifted and looked everywhere but her, Svana thought of their friendship, of how he found her mother and put himself between her and danger time and again. Watching the red still blaze on his cheeks, she considered her own heart, then smiled. "Bjorn." Svana took his hand and kissed his cheek. "You've given me more than I could ever hope for."

Bjorn's head popped up. After a moment, he grasped her hand back and leaned toward her.

"Ahem."

They jumped back to see Lord Magnar standing in the doorway. "It's time."

Svana nodded and headed inside. Stopping in the doorway, she glanced back at Bjorn. He smiled. As she reached to take Magnar's arm, she saw him glaring behind them at Bjorn. She jabbed him with her elbow, causing him to jump. He glanced between Svana and Bjorn, his features softening into reluctant acceptance.

Turning back one more time, he said to Bjorn, "If you hurt her, I'll have your head."

"Yes, sir."

Svana opened her mouth to speak but the two men nodded in understanding.

Magnar offered Svana his arm. She bit her lip then took it. *Let him protect you. Like a father with his daughter. If just for today.*

They made their way through the familiar corridors of Castle Alwilda to the large doors leading into the great hall. As they descended the stairs, she saw the other lords lined up, dressed in their finest, waiting to process in with her.

With a smile at each, Svana passed the lords as she took her position at the front of the line. As she waited for the doors to open, she let out a slow breath, hoping it would still her pounding heart. *No luck.*

Then, Magnar squeezed her hand and smiled at her. She hugged his arm and took a deep breath. Then she raised her chin and nodded.

The doors swung open as bagpipes blew, thundering across the room and shaking her to the core. Flower petals rained from the balconies above. The room was filled with people, squeezed in shoulder-to-shoulder in fine, colorful attire. All eyes were on Svana but she kept her focus straight ahead to her father's throne. As they ascended the dais, Lord Magnar squeezed her hand again, leaning in toward her like a hug. The lords spread out around behind her, surrounding her with their care and protection. And Bjorn stood close by. Behind the others but a constant presence.

And, perhaps, he'd stand by her side. Closing her eyes, she took in the warm, comforting presence, warming and protecting her like the thick fur of a bear.

Author's Note

My first introduction to fairy tales and how I formed my opinions of them was from my feelings toward the Disney films. I didn't read any of the actual stories until I was in my twenties. Which is why, to this day, one of my least liked fairy tales is *Snow White*.

So why on earth did I write a *Snow White* retelling?

It is all in thanks to the Rooglewood Fairy Tale contest. If you are familiar with Rooglewood, you probably know of or have read one or more of their *5 Something Something* anthologies. Each anthology included five novellas retelling a particular fairy tale. One was made for *Cinderella, Beauty and the* Beast, *Sleeping Beauty*, and, you guessed it, *Snow White*.

The *Snow White* theme was announced in 2017 and I worked from June to December getting my submission ready. It was set in feudal Japan with a daimyo's daughter and seven ronin. It ended up being a finalist in the contest but didn't win. Which was fair. It still needs work.

I know what you're saying. "Wait a second. I just read this book and it was not set in Japan."

That would be correct. Around the beginning of December, when I was supposed to be working on the second draft of my submission, I came up with the idea of crossing *Snow White* with *Goldie Locks* with a hint of Disney's *Brave* and started writing the opening chapter. At the time, I was more excited about this story than the one I was submitting. I had never written historical fiction before and I felt I was getting facts wrong so my confidence in my sub was way down. Fantasy was (is) my forte but I didn't have time to change so I put this story aside and finished and submitted my Japanese retelling for the contest. While it didn't win, I hope to publish it someday but first I feel I need to do more research.

So how did I end up returning to this version. Well, one day, I had many projects vying for my attention and I couldn't decide what to work on. Then I saw this premade cover by *Dragonpen Press*. Previously, I had played around with the idea of making my own covers (I will forever hire a cover artist, just saying) and had seen this model in stock photos and thought, "She would be great for this retelling," and filed the idea away. Now, here I was, staring at the very stock photo girl I wanted with an almost some green background and castle which was perfect for this story. I couldn't face anyone else buying it so… I did. Without a finished first draft. Or a title. That was toward the end of 2018. The plan was to write and publish this short novella in sixth months.

Three years later (wow, did it really take that long?) it is finally here. I so appreciate Savannah, my designer, waiting so patiently for me to finish the book so she could finish the cover and also for making it greener, adding the mist and bear to make it fit my story even more. It is gorgeous and I still melt over it.

I hope the story within does it justice.

But that is not the end of the story. You might be asking, "But why mix *Snow White* with *Goldie Locks?*"

Excellent question. It goes back to how this all started with my knowledge of the Disney version and no other. To avoid plagiarizing or basing my retelling off of Disney's movie, which can be very different from the originals, I read the Brothers Grimm tale while working on my Japanese retelling. When Snow White first arrives at the dwarfs' cottage, it is a very *Goldie Locks* scene, testing their food and beds for what she liked best. I thought it would be fun to mix the two and make the dwarfs bears instead. And *Brave* is one of my favorite Disney movies so that is why my heroine can fight and knows archery (that and I like writing heroines who can fight. My Japanese retelling also has my Snow White character fighting ninjas). Along the way, other fairy tales found their way into this one but the core is still *Snow White.*

This is why it is important never to stop at the movies. When a story is altered, either for film or for a retelling, things are lost or changed. Letting one source be the be-all, end-all means the full story is unknown. If I had never read the Brothers Grimm version, I never would have come up with this story. And if it wasn't for Rooglewood Press's contest, I may never have come up with my Japanese story, this one, or the THIRD(!) I hope to write someday.

Thank you for reading and I hope found something new within the pages that you never saw before.

Acknowledgements

To my friends and family: Thank you for reading my stuff and supporting my interests and letting me talk about my stories (if I was up to it).

To my online community (Realm Makers and Havok): Thank you for your support and being a place to connect with other writers and being such a great community. I've made friends and grown as a writer and just been able to enjoy hanging with others who understand the writer life.

To Selina Eckert: Thank you for Beta reading my novella. I appreciate all your comments and edits and the time you put into reading *The Beauty of Magic* when I know you had such a busy schedule.

To my mom: Thanks for always reading (and proofreading) my work. You make it look like I know what I'm doing when you catch those pesky, and obvious, typos.

To Deborah O'Carroll: Thank you for proofreading my novella. You caught so much that I had no idea I was doing wrong (or that I didn't know how to spell "lightning"). And your wonderful, encouraging comments. I laughed and smiled at so many of them and had to share with my mom.

To Savannah Jezowski: For the beautiful cover. It really makes the story shine and I still feel giddy when I look at it. And for your patience while I finished it. And for formatting the interior. You can do so much!

Finally, to God: Thank you for this talent and joy of writing. I don't think I would want any other gift. Of all the things I wanted to be when I grew up, who knew (besides you) this was the one that would stick. Because of this gift, I can be all those things and more, and hopefully create stories that inspire others as they have inspired me.

About the Author

Hailing from Minnesota, Rachel Ann Michael Harris has wanted to be everything from FBI agent, actress, search and rescue, dog handler, to teacher. But being a writer has been the only career that has stuck with her since childhood. She loved it so much that when she heard about a career where a degree in creative writing was acceptable, she was ready to jump. Double majoring in creative writing and communications, she graduated Magna Cum Laude and her first published work was a poem in her college's literary magazine. Since then, she's had numerous flash fiction stories published with *Havok Publishing* and is a contributor in several anthologies. She is currently working toward publishing her first full length novel. *The Beauty of Magic* is her first published novella.

When not writing, she is binge watching a favorite TV show, reading (hopefully) a good book, or doing one of these things when she should be writing.

If you want to keep up with her writing, reading, and dragons, follow her on Facebook, Instagram, or her website at **rachelannmichaelharris.wordpress.com**.